Skip School, Fly to Space

SKIP SCHOOL, FLY TO SPACE

llo My
me is Pig
WILLY
Rockitt
Shipp

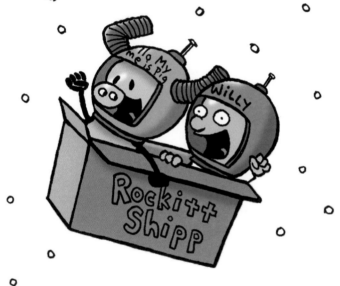

Stephan T. Pastis

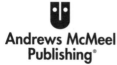

Andrews McMeel
Publishing®

Kansas City • Sydney • London

HEY THERE, RAT...WHAT DO YOU THINK OF MY NEW TANK TOP? I BOUGHT IT TO SHOW OFF MY NEW PHYSIQUE.
WHAT NEW PHYSIQUE?
I TOLD YOU. I'M AN ATHLETE NOW. EVEN THE DOCTOR CONFIRMED IT.
HE SAID YOU HAD ATHLETE'S FOOT.
HEY, IF I OIL UP, WILL YOU TAKE MY PICTURE?

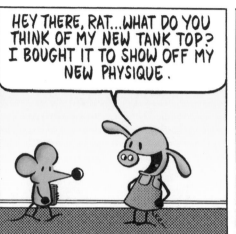

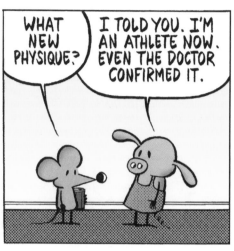

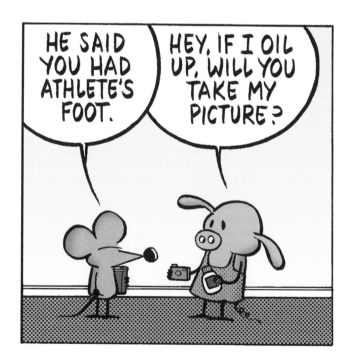

HEY, RAT... WHAT'S WITH THE SIGN?
IT'S MY SELF-AFFIRMATION POSTER. IT REMINDS ME WHERE I'M GOING IN LIFE.
Rat: Gravitating toward Greatness
OOOH... I WANT ONE... LIKE 'PIG: STRIVING FOR SUPER-NESS.'
NO NO NO... DUDE. YOUR AFFIRMATION QUOTE HAS TO BE REALISTIC... SOMETHING YOU CAN ACTUALLY ACHIEVE... HERE, TRY THIS ONE...
Pig: Leaning toward Loserville

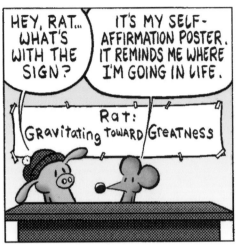

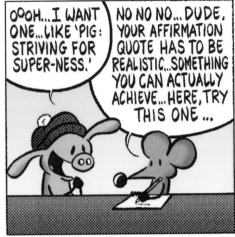

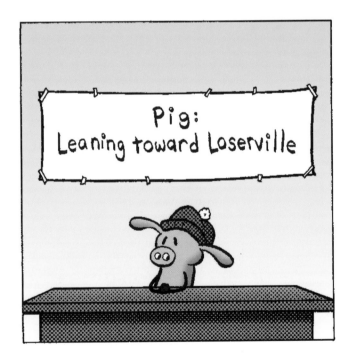

Okay, zeeba neighba.. Bob here spend day at city offices. He make 'connections.' Now crocs snap fingers...zeeba 'disappear.'
OH? WHAT KIND OF CONNECTIONS DID YOU MAKE?
Me got library card.
Sometimes me wish Bob disappear.

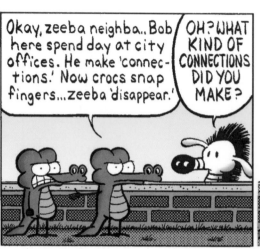

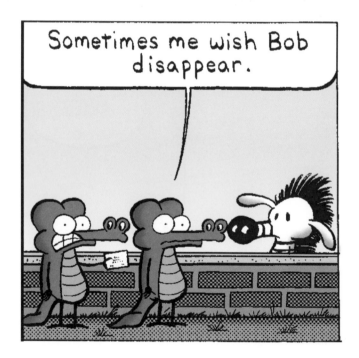

WHAT'S THAT BOOK ABOUT, RAT?
CRYOGENICS. IT'S THIS PROCESS WHERE THEY FREEZE DEAD GUYS SO THEY CAN DEFROST THEM LATER AND BRING THEM BACK TO LIFE.
AND THAT WORKS?
YEP.
ARISE.
HAM

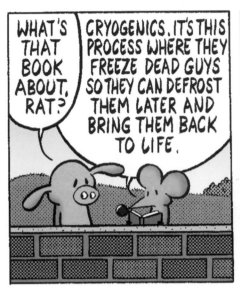

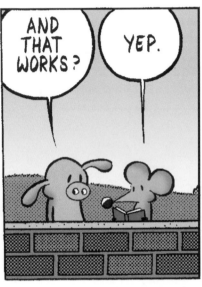

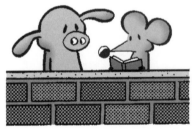

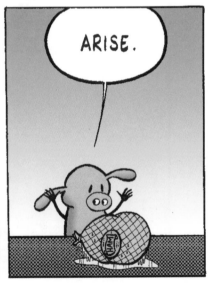

CAN I HELP YOU, SIR?
YES. THERE'S A PROBLEM WITH YOUR FILM AND YOUR PACKAGE SAYS MY SATISFACTION IS GUARANTEED.
FUJIDAK FILM Corporate Headquarters
WHAT'S THE PROBLEM?
WHEN I LOOK AT THE PHOTOS IN MY ALBUM, THEY'RE FILLED WITH PEOPLE WHO ARE NO LONGER AROUND AND FRIENDS WHO ARE NO LONGER FRIENDS AND HOMES I CAN NO LONGER GET BACK TO.
I'M AFRAID THAT'S JUST LIFE, SIR.
I'M NOT SATISFIED.

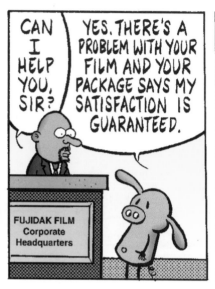

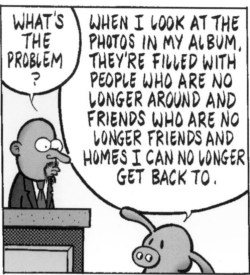

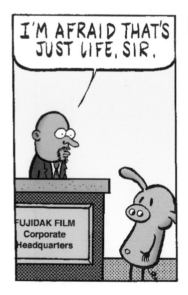

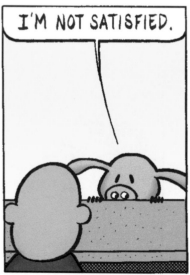

HEY, RAT.. MIND IF I BORROW THIS CARDBOARD BOX I FOUND IN YOUR CLOSET? I'M STARTING A BLOG.
A BLOG? WHAT DO YOU NEED A BOX FOR IF YOU'RE DOING A BLOG?
FOR ALL THE MONEY I'M GONNA MAKE.

ARE THERE INTERVENTIONS FOR STUPIDITY?

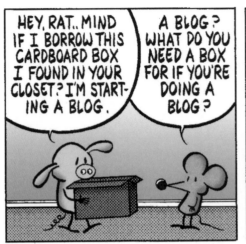

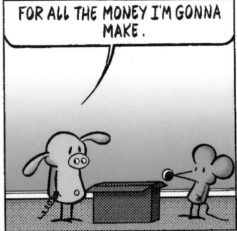

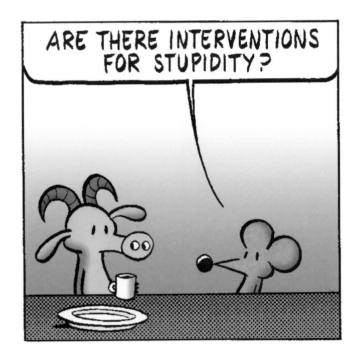

I SAW THE MOST INSPIRING MOVIE LAST NIGHT.
WHAT WAS IT?
'KARATE KID.'
'KARATE KID'? WHAT KIND OF LOSER GETS INSPIRED BY A TWENTY-YEAR-OLD KARATE FILM?

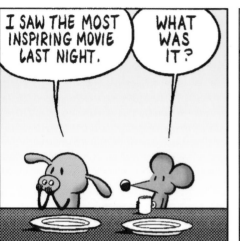

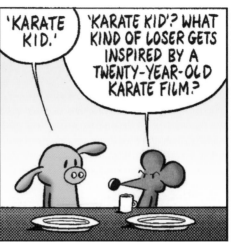

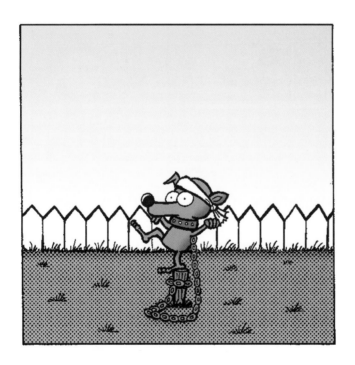

Hulloo°oo, zeeba neighba... Leesten, me hear you lose tooth.
YEAH, I FELL IN THE KITCHEN AND KNOCKED IT OUT. WHY ARE YOU ASKING?
Ohhhh, no reeson. Me is juss, like, want be gud neighba.
WHATEVER.

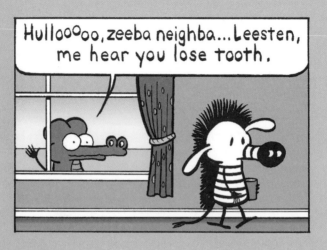

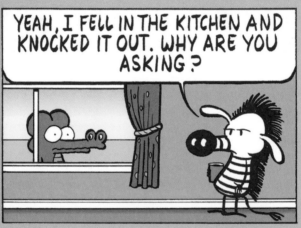

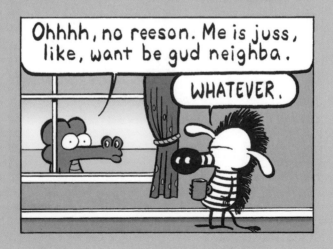

Oh, well... Now me know you okay, me guess me juss leave and—
HOLY SMOKE! ZEEBA NEIGHBA! IS TOOTH FAIRY! OPEN DOOR! GET MONIES!
Look like someone no beleeve in tooth fairy.

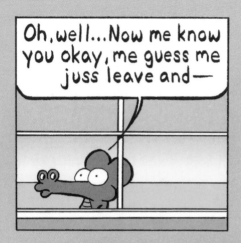

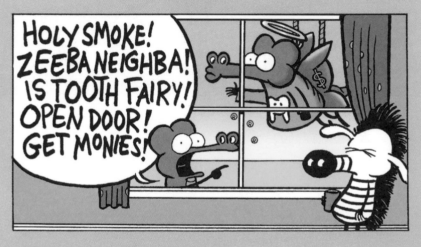

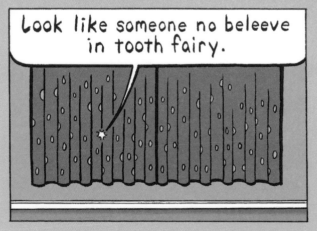

Hey, son. Whuh you reading?
'ROMEO AND JULIET.'.. IT'S FOR MY ENGLISH CLASS.
Oh, yeah? Read me leetle bit.
'LO, HERE UPON THY CHEEK THE STAIN DOTH SIT OF AN OLD TEAR THAT IS NOT WASH'D OFF YET. IF E'ER THOU WAST THYSELF AND THESE WOES THINE, THOU AND THESE WOES WERE ALL FOR ROSALINE.'
Dis might be gud time drop out of school.

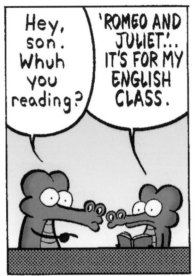

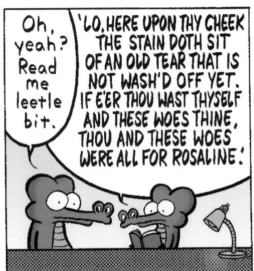

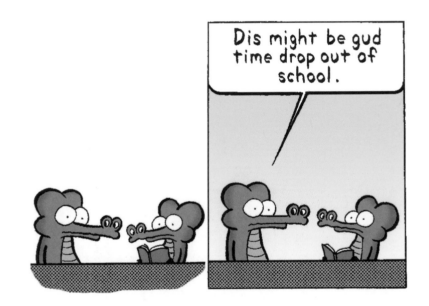

Okay, zeeba, crocs has new strategy. We ees prove we tough by keeling Bob.
Yeah. So een future when we hunt, you ees juss fall down een fear.
Uh. You no have future, Bob.
Me starting rethink strategy, Fred.

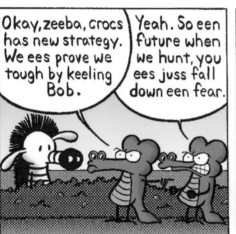

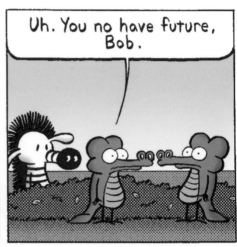

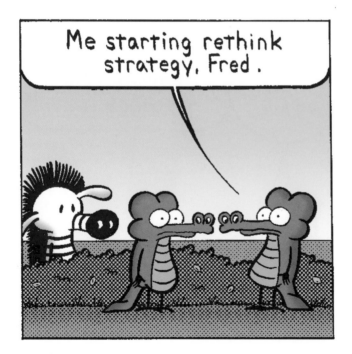

PIG, YOU AND I HAVE BEEN ARGUING A LOT LATELY. I THINK IT'S TIME WE TRY TO REACH A FAIR CONSENSUS.
WHAT'S A CONSENSUS ?
IT'S WHERE WE GET TOGETHER AND I STATE MY OPINION AND YOU STATE YOUR OPINION AND THEN WE AGREE TO MY OPINION.
THAT DOESN'T SEEM FAIR.
BELIEVE ME... I LISTEN CAREFULLY TO YOUR OPINION BEFORE I MOCK IT.

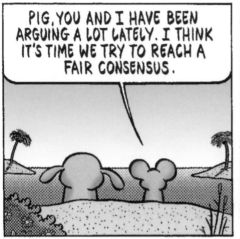

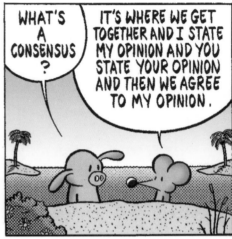

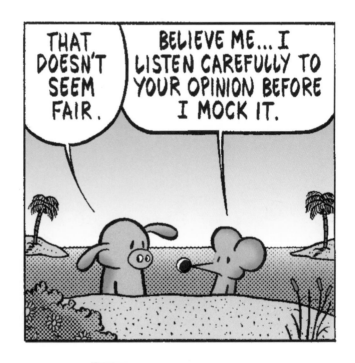

OKAY, GUYS, IT SEEMS LIKE WITH OIL, FOOD AND ALL THE OTHER WORLD'S COMMODITIES, NEWSPAPER INK IS NOW IN SHORT SUPPLY.
SO?
SO THAT MEANS CUTBACKS. LIKE TODAY, NO PANEL LINES.
THAT'S NOT SO BAD. CAN WE DO ANYTHING ELSE?
NEXT TIME KEEP YOUR FAT MOUTH SHUT.
LOOK! MY IDEAL BODY WEIGHT!

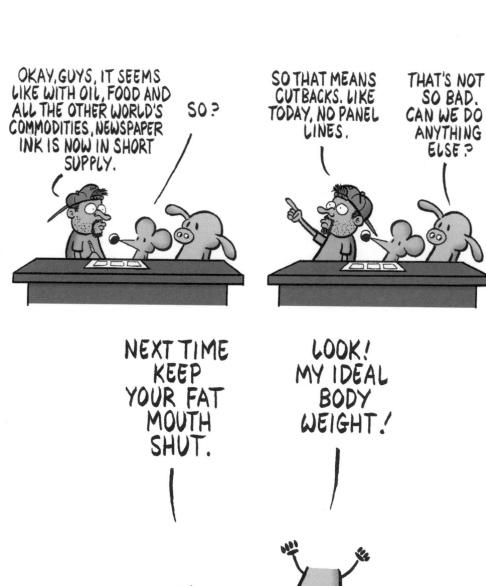

WHY ARE YOU SITTING IN A BUCKET?
BECAUSE THE WORLD IS ENDING AND I WANT TO SURVIVE.
WHAT WILL SITTING IN A BUCKET DO?
WHENEVER YOU SEE PICTURES OF A TRAGEDY, NONE OF THE VICTIMS ARE EVER SITTING IN A BUCKET.
SO?
SO GUYS WHO SIT IN BUCKETS MUST DO FINE.
PERHAPS I CHOSE A BAD BUCKET.

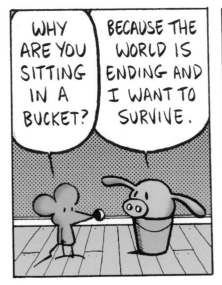

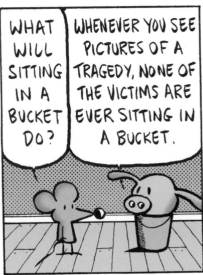

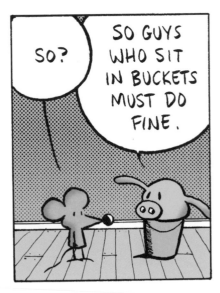

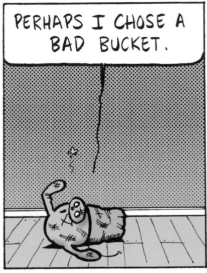

WHAT ARE YOU DOING, RAT?

I AM CARRYING AROUND A WINDOW. I CALL IT 'STEP ONE' OF MY GRAND PLAN TO ISOLATE MYSELF FROM A WORLD I DO NOT LIKE.

BUT HOW CAN YOU DO THAT? THE WORLD IS FILLED WITH SO MANY INTERESTING PEOPLE..PEOPLE WHO'D LIKE TO MEET YOU..PEOPLE WHO'D LIKE TO TALK TO YOU...

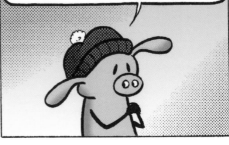

I CALL THIS 'STEP TWO.'

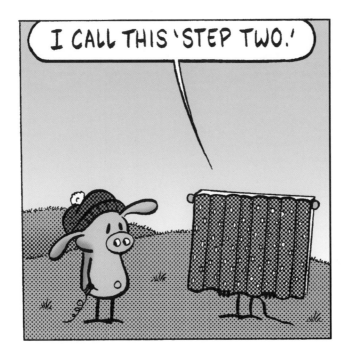

WHAT ARE YOU DOING, PIG?
I HAVE TO GIVE A SPEECH NEXT WEEK, SO I'M PRACTICING IT IN FRONT OF THE MIRROR TO BUILD UP MY CONFIDENCE.
WHY BOTHER? YOU STINK.
IT'S NOT HELPING.

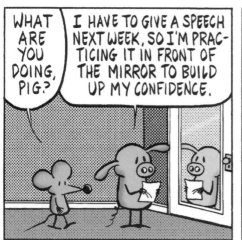

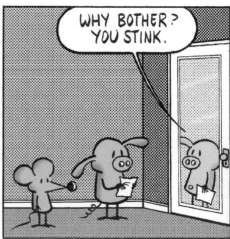

Whuh you watching, Larry ?
Some kind nature show, but me no unnerstann.
Whuh you no unner-stann ?
Dese beeg beast guys fight for terrytory, but no one bother eet striped guys running round.
IT'S CALLED FOOTBALL, DAD. AND YOU CAN'T EAT THE REFEREES.
What point of dat?
Laaaame.

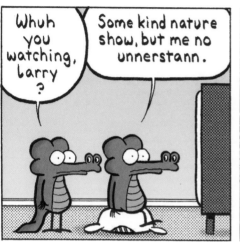

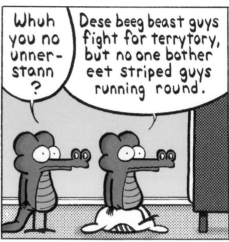

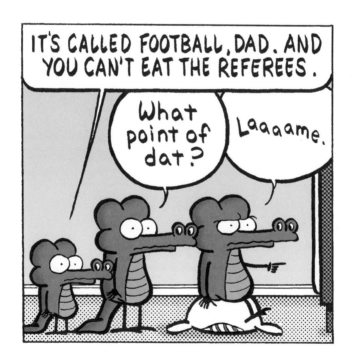

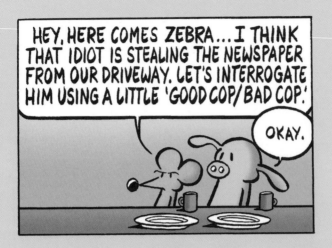

HEY, HERE COMES ZEBRA...I THINK THAT IDIOT IS STEALING THE NEWSPAPER FROM OUR DRIVEWAY. LET'S INTERROGATE HIM USING A LITTLE 'GOOD COP/BAD COP.'

OKAY.

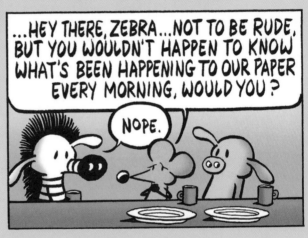

...HEY THERE, ZEBRA...NOT TO BE RUDE, BUT YOU WOULDN'T HAPPEN TO KNOW WHAT'S BEEN HAPPENING TO OUR PAPER EVERY MORNING, WOULD YOU?

NOPE.

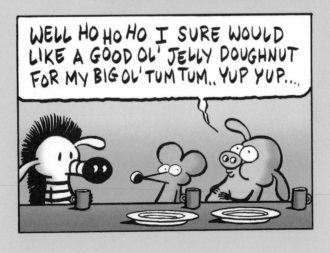

WELL HO HO HO I SURE WOULD LIKE A GOOD OL' JELLY DOUGHNUT FOR MY BIG OL' TUM TUM.. YUP YUP....

PIG?
YES?
IT'S GOOD COP/BAD COP...
NOT GOOD COP/*FAT* COP.
OH.
I AM SO CONFUSED.
I AM SO ANGRY.
I AM SOOOO HUNGRY.

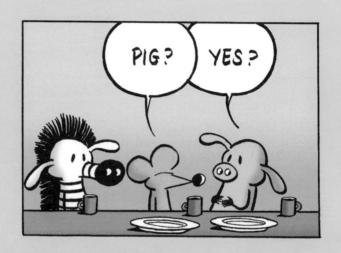

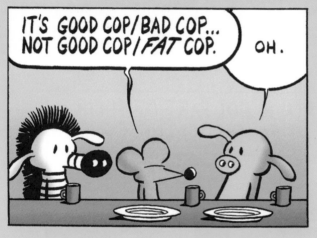

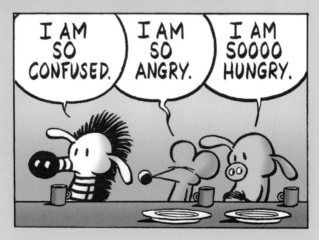

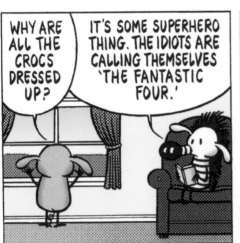

WHY ARE ALL THE CROCS DRESSED UP?

IT'S SOME SUPERHERO THING. THE IDIOTS ARE CALLING THEMSELVES 'THE FANTASTIC FOUR.'

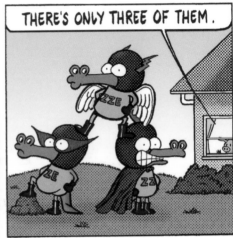

THERE'S ONLY THREE OF THEM.

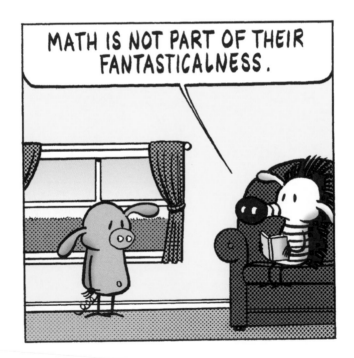

MATH IS NOT PART OF THEIR FANTASTICALNESS.

Okay, if we ees be superhero, we ees need super special skills. You know, like ability lift earth, breathe fire, freeze oceans, catch bullets.
Me is clear paper jams.
Dat pretty special.

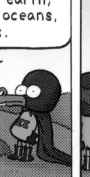

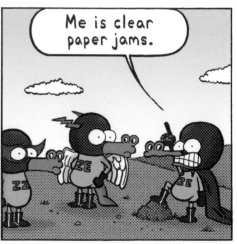

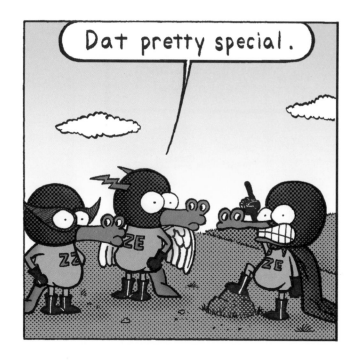

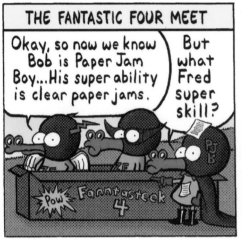

THE FANTASTIC FOUR MEET
Okay, so now we know Bob is Paper Jam Boy...His super ability is clear paper jams.
But what Fred super skill?
PJB
ZF
POW
Fanntasteck 4
Me not know. How you plan save earth, Fred?
How? Me tell you how. What if after Bob clear papers from paper jam, dey ees blow everywhere, but Bob needed dem stay togedder in nice neat, original order?
ZF
And thus was born Stapler Head.
SH

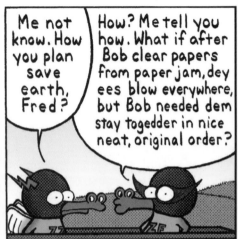

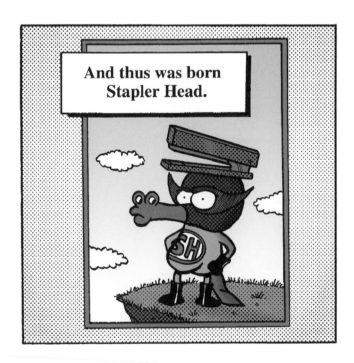

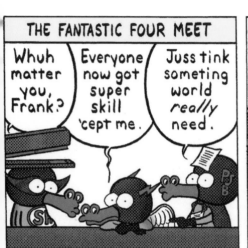

THE FANTASTIC FOUR MEET

Whuh matter you, Frank?

Everyone now got super skill 'cept me.

Juss tink someting world *really* need.

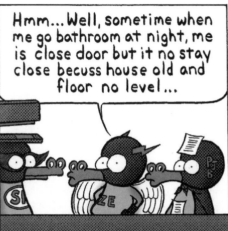

Hmm... Well, sometime when me go bathroom at night, me is close door but it no stay close becuss house old and floor no level...

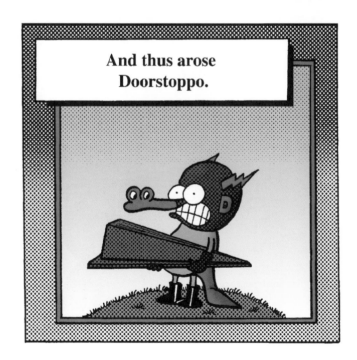

And thus arose Doorstoppo.

THE FANTASTIC FOUR MEET
Okay, if we ees all be on same superteam, we ees all need learn leetle bit 'bout other guy's skills. Paper Jam Boy, how is you clear paper jams?
POW
Ohhhhh... Dat pretty involved. You really want know?
We really want know.

BOOT
BOOT
BOOT

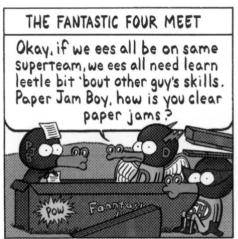

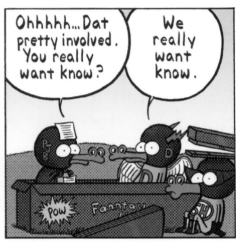

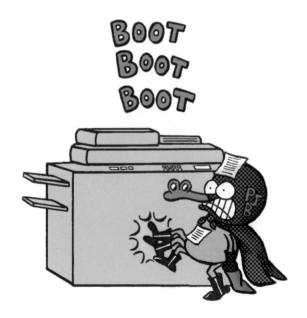

HEY, RAT...I'D LIKE YOU TO MEET MY FRIEND, BOB...HE WORKS IN CONSTRUCTION.
WHAT DO YOU BUILD?
HOUSES.
FROM THE GROUND UP?
CEILING DOWN.
BUSINESS IS REALLY DROPPING.

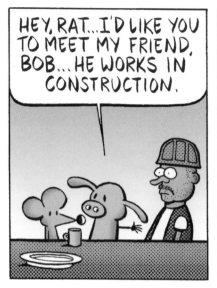

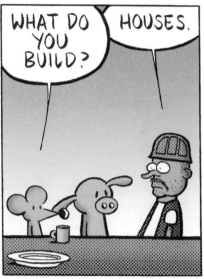

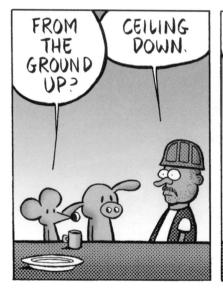

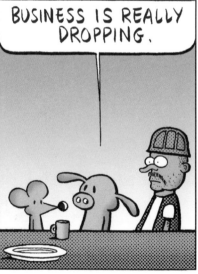

Whuh ees you reading son?
A BOOK ON MARTIN LUTHER KING, JR... I'M TRYING TO READ BOOKS ABOUT ALL MY HEROES, LIKE KING AND LINCOLN AND GANDHI AND TOLSTOY.
HEH HEH HEH... Ohhhhh, son... You call *dem* heroes ??
OF COURSE I CALL THEM HEROES. WHO DO *YOU* CONSIDER HEROES ?

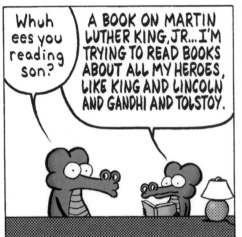

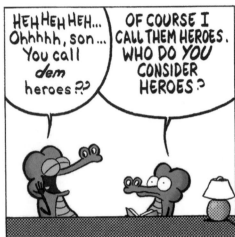

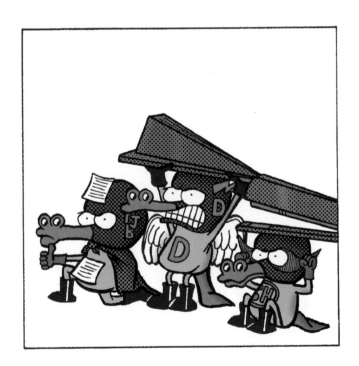

I'VE DECIDED TO START SAYING SORRY FOR ALL THE WRONGS I'VE COMMITTED AGAINST OTHERS.
BECAUSE YOU'VE REALIZED ALL THE PAIN YOU'VE CAUSED?
BECAUSE I'VE REALIZED SORRY IS JUST A WORD AND YOU CAN SAY IT WITHOUT MEANING IT.
THAT'S NOT NICE.
SORRY.

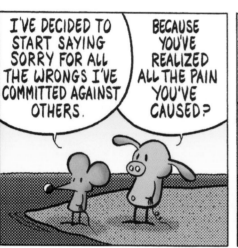

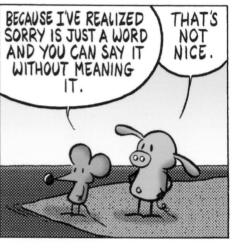

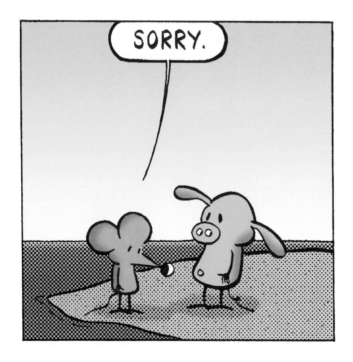

HI.
HI. DO I KNOW YOU?
WELL.. HEH HEH.. YOU MIGHT... I'M THE GUY WHO WRITES THAT BLOG.
WHAT BLOG?
THE ONE ON THE WORLD WIDE WEB.
THEY'RE *ALL* ON THE WEB.
OH. MINE IS THE ONE WITH *LINKS*.
THEY'VE *ALL* GOT LINKS.
THEY DO?

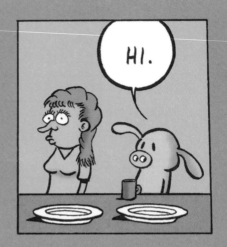

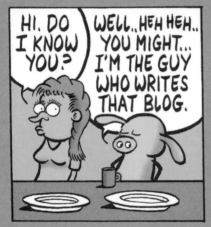

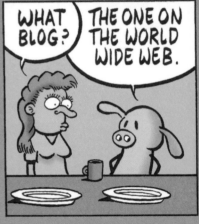

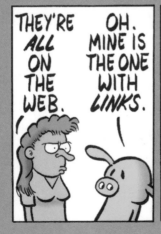

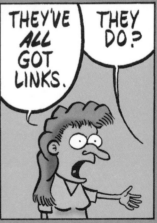

YES!
AND A SECTION ABOUT THE AUTHOR?
YES!
AND POSTINGS WITH CLEVER LITTLE INSIGHTS?
YES!
AHA!!
'AHA' WHAT?
MINE AREN'T CLEVER.
OH, LORD.
HI... I'M THAT UNCLEVER GUY ON THE INTERNET.

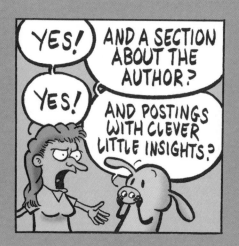

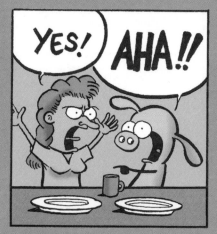

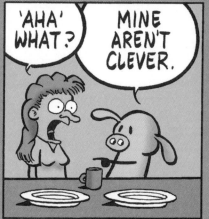

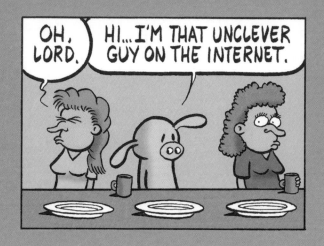

HOW DOES YOUR HEART KNOW TO KEEP BEATING WHEN YOU'RE ASLEEP?
YOUR SUBCONSCIOUS HANDLES IT, UNLESS YOUR CONSCIOUS MIND STARTS TO FOCUS IN ON IT. THEN YOU CREATE 'UTTER BRAIN CHAOS.' SO IT'S BETTER NOT TO THINK ABOUT IT.
WHY DO YOU TELL HIM STUFF LIKE THAT?
BECAUSE IT'S FUN AND BESIDES, EVEN A MORON LIKE PIG KNOWS WHEN HE'S BEING MESSED WITH.
3:04

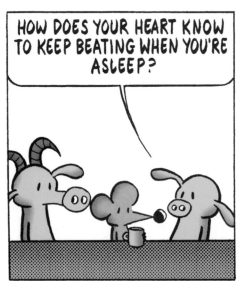

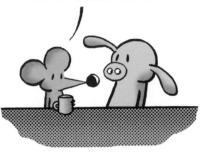

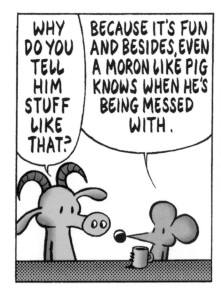

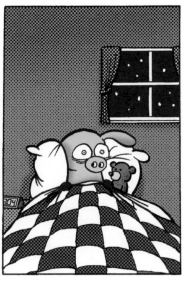

THIS SURE IS A TERRIFIC HISTORY BOOK... IT'S CALLED 'THE GREAT INFLUENZA' BY JOHN BARRY.
OH, BOY... DOES IT MENTION MY GRANDMA?
DID SHE DIE?
NO. BUT SHE HAD A GREAT INFLUENZA ON MY LIFE.
IT WAS A PLAGUE, PIG.
PLEASE DON'T INSULT MY GRANDMA.

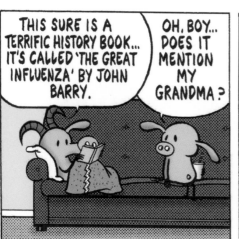

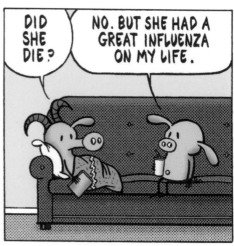

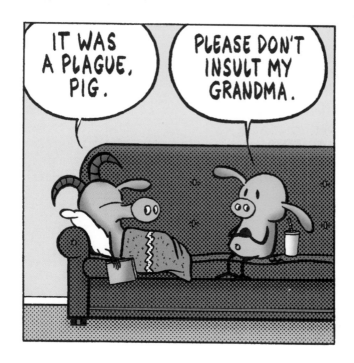

Dear Pigita,
I have problems.
I have insecurities.
Please date me anyways.
YOU DUMB PIG...GIRLS ARE ATTRACTED TO CONFIDENCE.
I THOUGHT THAT WAS BAD... I THOUGHT THAT MEANT YOU HAD A BIG HEAD.
THAT'S ARROGANCE... CONFIDENCE IS SOMETHING LESS. SHOW HER YOU HAVE IT.
I have a medium-sized head.

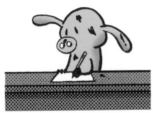

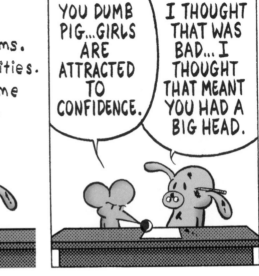

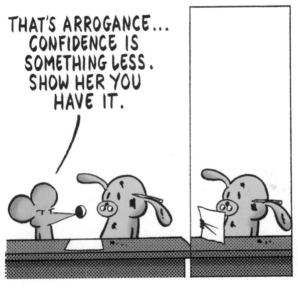

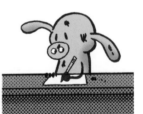

DUDE, WHAT'S THAT SMELL?
OH, IT'S PROBABLY ME. THERE'S A DROUGHT, SO I'VE STOPPED SHOWERING.
SO WHAT ARE YOU GONNA DO—JUST GO AROUND SMELLING AWFUL?!
OH, NO, NO, SILLY, EVERY FIFTEEN MINUTES, I RUB 'SPEED STICK' ALL OVER MY FACE.
DUDE.
Mmmmmmmm Feels gooooooood.

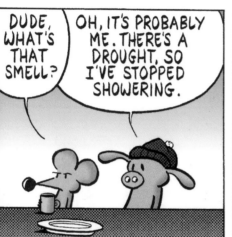

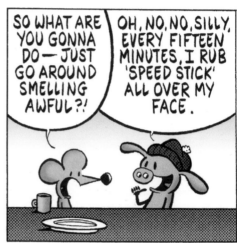

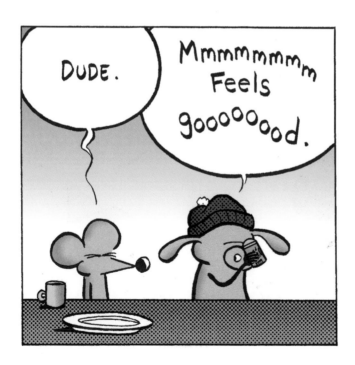

HAPPY BIRTHDAY TO YOU
HAPPY BIRTHDAY TO YOU
HAPPY BIRTHDAY TO—
LAAAARRY!
Me can't hear you
Me can't hear you
Me can't hear you
NOT HEARING YOUR NAME SUNG DOESN'T MEAN YOU DON'T AGE A YEAR, DAD.
Twenty-seex *AGAIN*... WOOHOO!

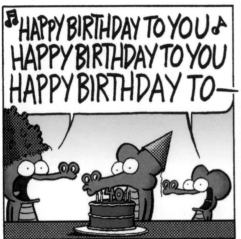

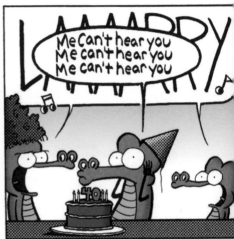

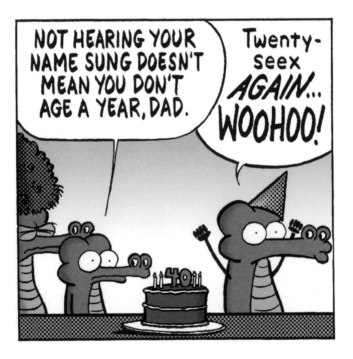

WHAT'S THE MATTER WITH YOU, DAD?
Me turn forty. Me spose keel billion zeebas by now. Me waste whole life.
DAD, YOU HAVEN'T WASTED EVERY MOMENT OF YOUR LIFE JUST BECAUSE YOU HAVEN'T CAUGHT ALL THE ZEBRAS YOU THOUGHT YOU'D CATCH. I CAN THINK OF A MILLION OF THOSE MOMENTS YOU DIDN'T WASTE.
Oh yeah? Like wheech ones?

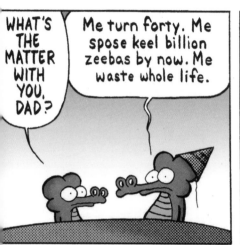

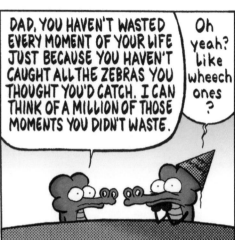

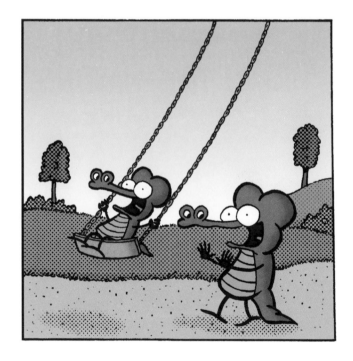

WHAT ARE YOU WATCHING, RAT?
HOCKEY.
I DIDN'T KNOW YOU LIKED HOCKEY.
I LOVE HOCKEY...EXCEPT FOR THESE BORING LITTLE INTERLUDES WHERE THEY SKATE AROUND TRYING TO HIT THAT BLACK THING.
THE PUCK.
FIGHT, YOU TIME-WASTING FIGURE SKATERS!!!

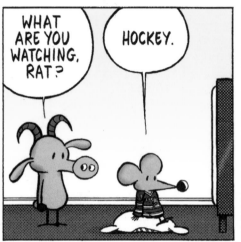

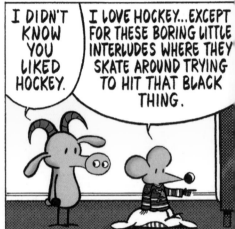

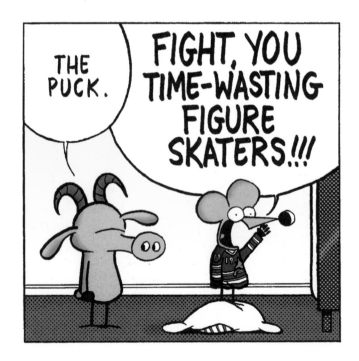

HEY, GOAT, HAVE YOU EVER HEARD OF A SUPER STRONG GUY NAMED SAMSON WHOSE STRENGTH WAS ALL IN HIS HAIR?
YEAH. HIS WIFE DELILAH CUT IT AND HE LOST ALL HIS POWER. WHY?
NO REASON.
MULLETS DO NOT GIVE SUPERPOWERS.

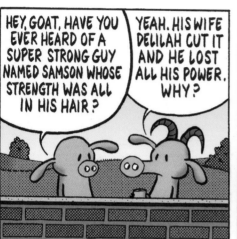

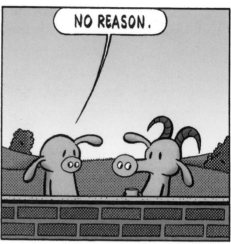

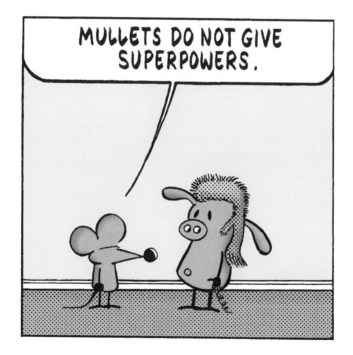

WHAT ARE YOU DOING?
Crocs do 'Shakespeares For Da Masses.' Me reecite Shakespeares in oreeginal language and Bob follow wid translation for modern audience. Have leesten...
Ahem
'Friends, Romans, Countrymen, lend me your ears.'

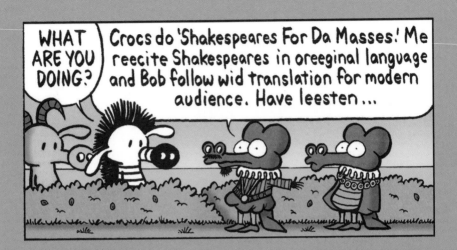

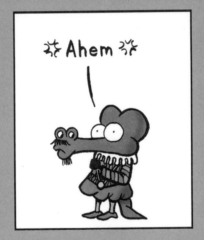

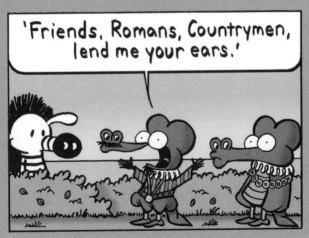

'SHUT YOU FAT MOUF!'
I THINK IT LOSES SOMETHING.
Hey... you not shutting mouf.

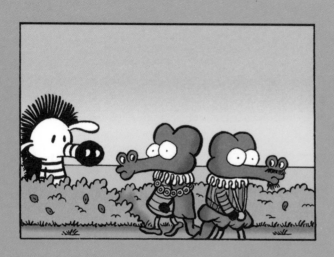

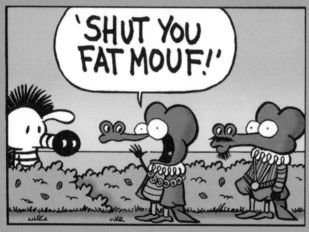

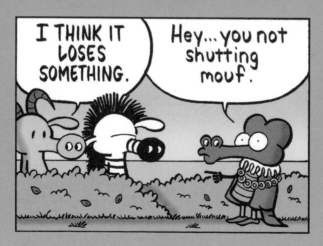

IF EVERY LIFE IS SACRED, WHY DO WE KILL EACH OTHER IN WARS?
BECAUSE SOME LIFE IS SACREDER THAN OTHERS.
WHOSE LIFE IS SACREDER?
PEOPLE WHO AGREE WITH YOU.
I DON'T GET IT.
I SUGGEST YOU AGREE.
OKAY DOKE.

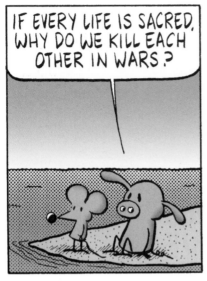

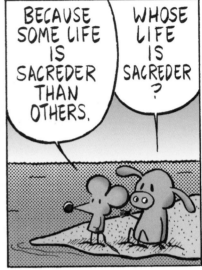

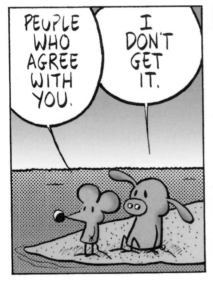

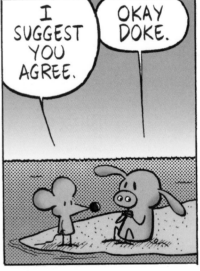

HAVE YOU SEEN YOUR FATHER?
HE'S OUTSIDE. I HAVE TO DO A PROJECT FOR BIOLOGY WHERE I FIND AND CATALOG TWENTY DIFFERENT BIRDS. DAD'S BIRDWATCHING FOR ME.
JUNIOR! JUNIOR! Me find one!
TERRIFIC, DAD! DESCRIBE ITS PHYSICAL CHARACTERISTICS AND I'LL TRY TO FIND IT IN THE BIRD GUIDE.
Uhh. Two wings. Lotta feathers.
YOU NEED TO BE A LITTLE MORE SPECIFIC, DAD.
Oh, yeah. It have head.

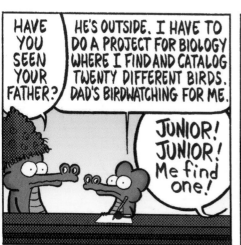

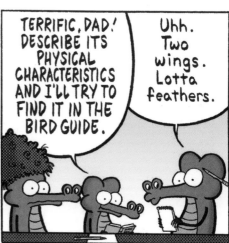

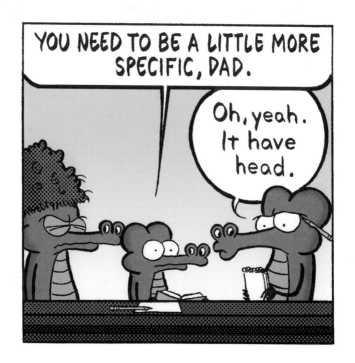

WOO HOO!
WHAT?
I JUST SCOURED THE 'GUINNESS BOOK OF WORLD RECORDS' AND NOTICED THERE IS NO RECORD HOLDER IN THE CATEGORY OF 'MOST CONSECUTIVE TIMES SLAPPING YOUR ROTUND FRIEND IN THE FACE'!
WOO HOO!
I'M HAVING SECOND THOUGHTS.

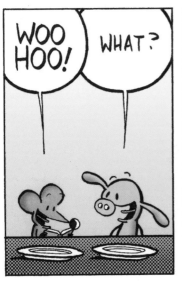

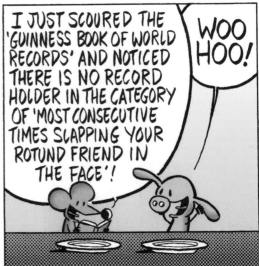

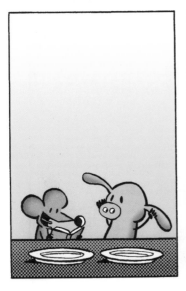

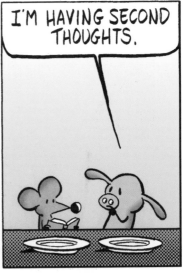

PIG MADE FRIENDS WITH A HIPPO.
A HIPPO? WHY A HIPPO?

HE SAID BECAUSE HIPPOS HAVE BIG, SOFT, JIGGLY ARMS, LIKE HIS GRANDMA USED TO HAVE.
WHAT'S THE IMPORTANCE OF BIG, SOFT, JIGGLY ARMS?

ZZZZZZZZ

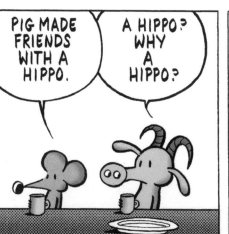

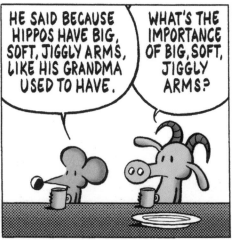

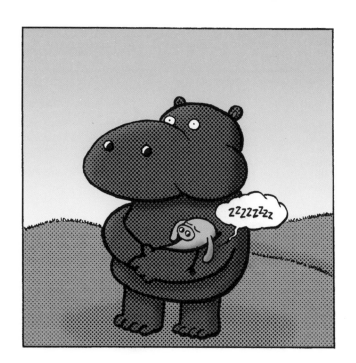

WHAT ARE YOU TWO DOING?
Shut mouf. We is ninja. We is have poison dart here eenside dart gun. We blow at zeeba. Keel you.
Bob...No use poison dart gun dreenk milkshake.
SLUUUURP
What waste of milkshake.

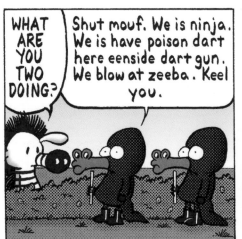

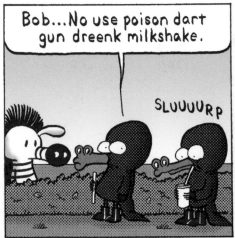

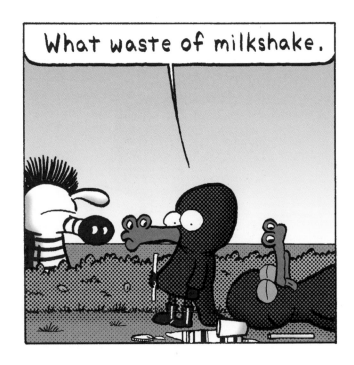

TONIGHT ON THE NEWS AT TEN... WAR
Famine
Death
Hate
Lies
Bad
Bad
Bad
Bad
Worse
Worser

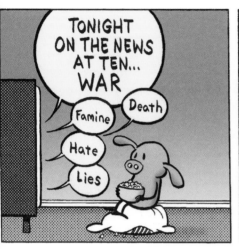

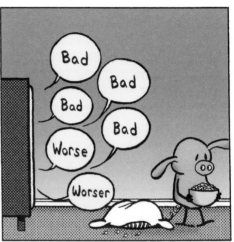

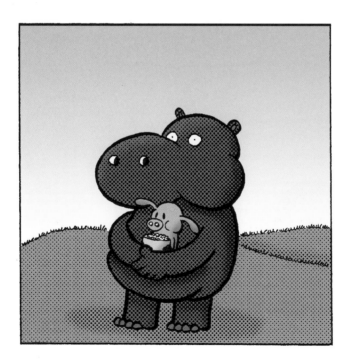

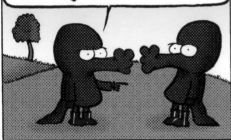

Okay, neenjas, leesten...First key to neenja assasseen ees neenja stealth. Dat mean neenjas no make sound and no carry nutteeng dat might *make* sound...

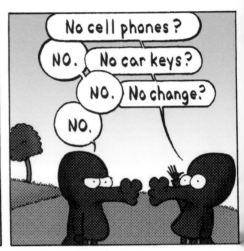

No cell phones?

NO.

No car keys?

NO.

No change?

NO.

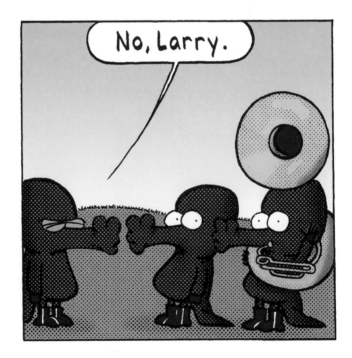

No, Larry.

HEY, MOM... DAD WANTS TO KNOW IF YOU'VE SEEN HIS 'SUPER STEALTHY NINJA' COSTUME.. HE AND THE OTHER CROCS ARE SNEAKING UP ON SOME ZEBRA'S HOUSE TONIGHT.
I WASHED IT WITH THE LOAD OF WHITES I DID TODAY.
THE WHITES? DON'T YOU SOMETIMES PUT BLEACH ON THOSE?
YEAH. SO?

Go home, Larry.

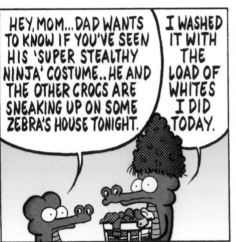

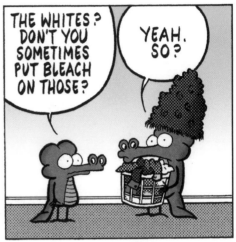

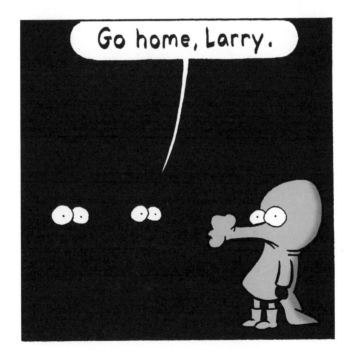

Whuh matter you, woomun?
STUPID PRINTER'S NOT WORKING. IT'S OUT OF INK.
PFOO PFOO PFOO PFOO
PJB
PAPER JAM BOY!
It ees me.
PJB
Spidey-sense tell me you has paper jam.
NO. WE HAVE AN EMPTY PRINTER CARTRIDGE.
PJB

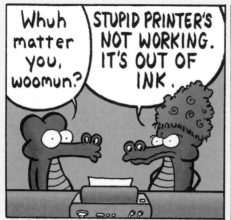

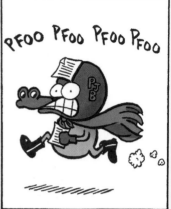

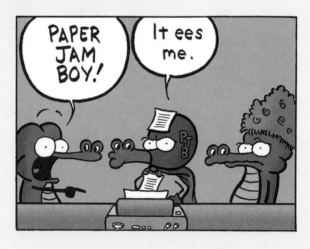

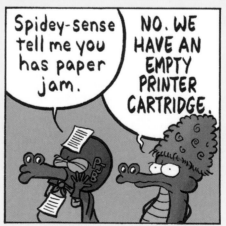

Preenter cartridge? Dat like sooo esspensive...Such reep-off...And me no has power to feex...Oh, no... Me fading fast... Look... like... evil.... preenter......
...defeet me.
THUD!
YOUR SUPERHERO IS SOMETHING LESS THAN SUPER.
CURSE YOU, EVIL HOOLITT PACKURD!!!

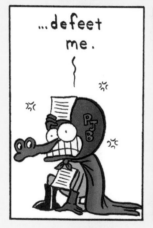

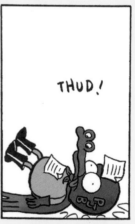

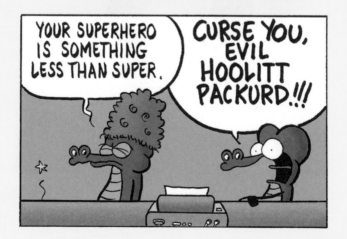

Me kicking you out of neenjas, Larry. You lame. You no smart.
Me no smart? HA! Like, look een mirror, Frank.
Okay, like, now you reelly out.
Fine. Me no care. Larry no need you stoopid uneeform. Larry got udder frends. Tougher den stoopid neenjas. Cooler den stoopid neenjas.

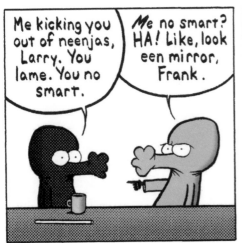

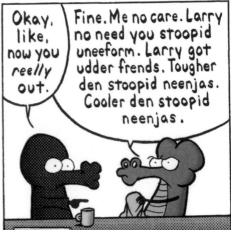

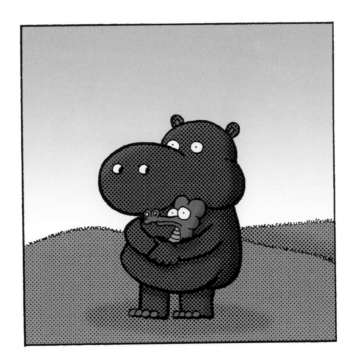

RAT, I'D LIKE YOU TO MEET MY COUSIN SQUIDMO...HE'S A PROFESSIONAL ZEBRA RIGHTS ACTIVIST WHO'S DEDICATED HIS LIFE TO DRAFTING VARIOUS METHODOLOGIES FOR KEEPING ZEBRAS SAFE FROM PREDATORS.
OH, YEAH? LET ME HEAR ONE.
"RUN."
SQUIDMO MAY NOT BE GIVING YOU YOUR MONEY'S WORTH.

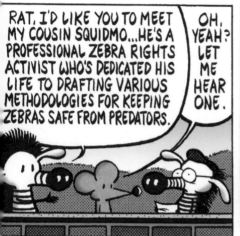

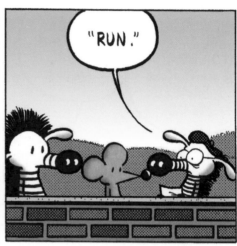

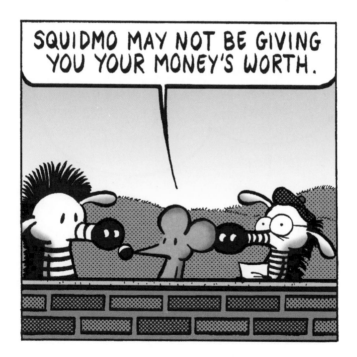

HEY, DAD...CAN YOU TAKE ME TO 'GAMESTOP'? I WANT TO GET A GAME FOR MY DS.
No. Me glue head to wall.
WHY'D YOU DO THAT?!
Personal goal.
MAYBE I'LL JUST ASK MOM.
Reemember, son... Always set goals een life.

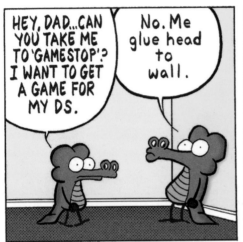

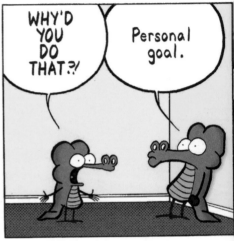

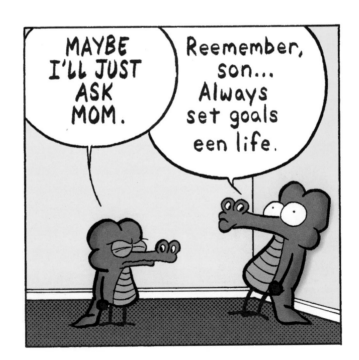

HIYA, RAT... WHATCHA EATING?
DONUTS. WANT ONE?
DONUTS
I'D LOVE ONE.
DONUTS
LICK LICK LICK LICK LICK LICK
I'VE CHANGED MY MIND.
CAN'T SAY I DIDN'T OFFER.
DONUTS

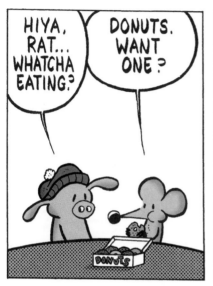

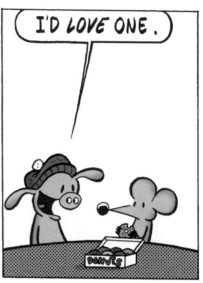

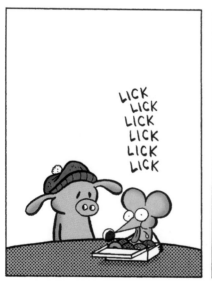

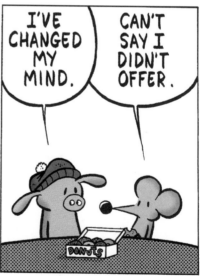

I'M FASCINATED BY SLEEP.
WHY IS THAT?
BECAUSE IT'S SO MYSTERIOUS...I MEAN, WHERE DOES OUR MIND GO? WHY DO WE DREAM? AND WHY DO WE DREAM *WHAT* WE DREAM? IS THAT OTHER WORLD REAL? ARE WE COMMUNICATING WITH OTHERS?... IT'S JUST SUCH A FASCINATING MYSTERY. DON'T YOU THINK?
ZZZZZZ
SNORRRRRRR

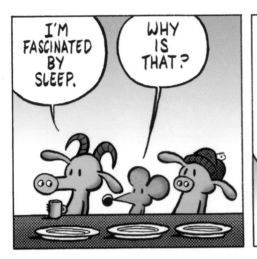

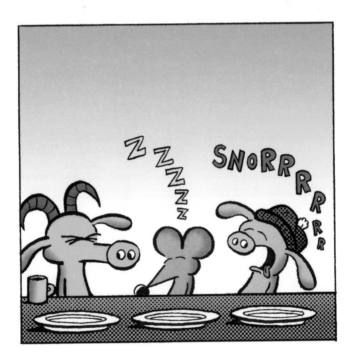

LOOK AT THIS STORY FROM NEW ZEALAND...A MAN GOT ARRESTED FOR ASSAULTING ANOTHER MAN WITH A HEDGEHOG. CAN YOU IMAGINE VENTING YOUR ANGER BY THROWING A HEDGE-HOG AT SOMEONE? ISN'T THAT RIDICULOUS?
DID YOU EAT MY LAST 'DING DONG'?

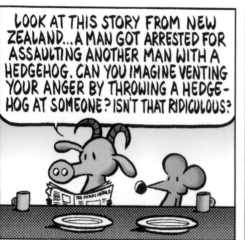

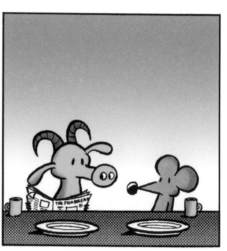

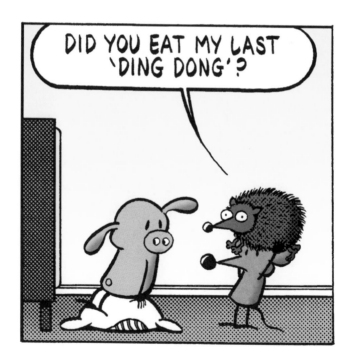

BOMBAST CABLE... CAN I HELP YOU?
YOU WEASELS RAISED MY CABLE BILL AGAIN. LOWER IT NOW OR FACE MY WRATH.
I'M SORRY, SIR, BUT I BELIEVE WE'RE THE ONLY CABLE COMPANY IN YOUR AREA, SO I'M AFRAID YOU DON'T HAVE A LOT OF OPTIONS.
OH, I'VE GOT OPTIONS.

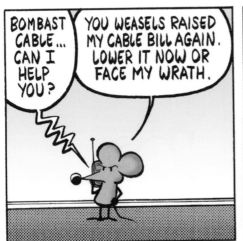

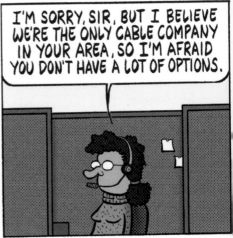

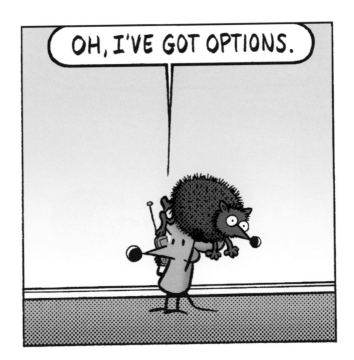

Hey, son... Leesten dis news me juss see in paper... Twenty-four percent of college gradueetes is have trubble find jobs.
SO?
SO JUNIOR HIGH BEEG WASTE OF TIME!!!
THANKS FOR THE ACADEMIC ENCOURAGEMENT, DAD.
No use beeg words, son. Dey for loosers.

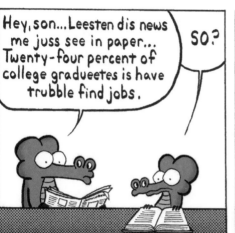

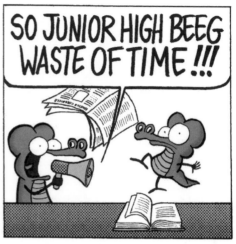

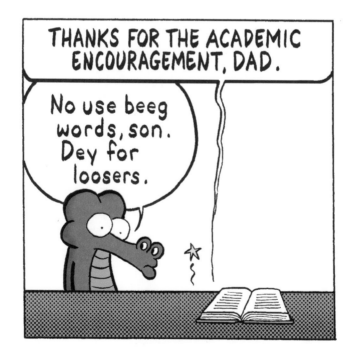

♫
HAIL TO CHEEF!!
WHAT ARE YOU DOING?
Crocs geet Pressydent of United State to take side of crocs. Now he geev speech. Order bad tings for you sad zeeba face!
I FIND IT HARD TO BELIEVE YOU EVEN KNOW WHO THE PRESIDENT IS.
Beeg important man. Whole country like. Geevs gud speeches. From some place called Eelinoise.

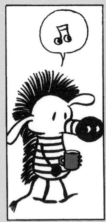

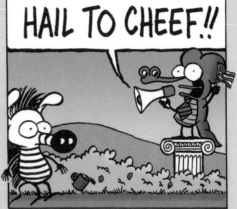

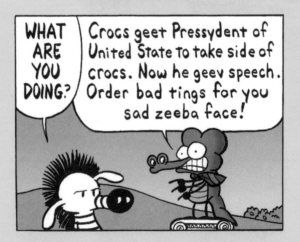

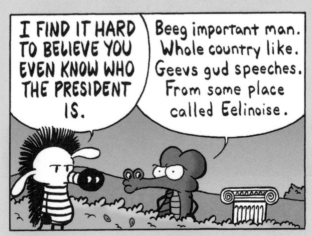

ALRIGHT, FINE...SO YOU KNOW CURRENT EVENTS. IT HARDLY MEANS YOU COULD GET HIM TO ———
FOUR SCORED AND SEVEN YEAR AGO!!!
OHHHHH, LORD.
Hey, shut mouf. Leesten to Pressydent Leencoln-Log.
Blah blah blah Okay... Where part me aboleesh zeeb-ery?

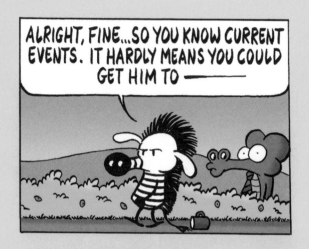

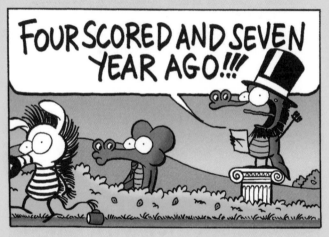

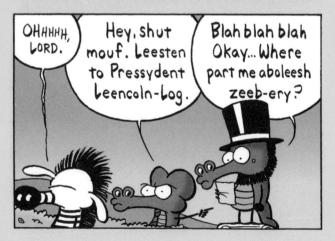

WHAT ARE YOU DOING, PIG?
I GOT A JOB. I STAND ON THE SIDEWALK AND HOLD A SIGN.
NEW HOMES
NEW HOMES
MY MAMA RAISED A POLE.
NEW HOMES

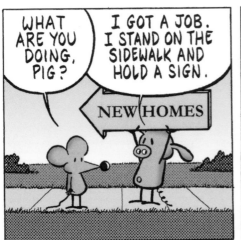

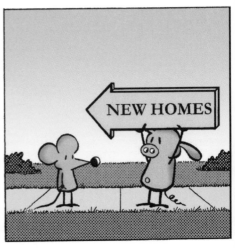

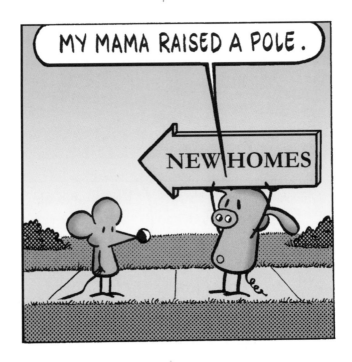

EVERY TIME I STARE AT MY REFLECTION IN THE MIRROR, I FEEL SO FAT AND DUMPY.
OH, PIG, WHY?
WHY? LOOK AT HIM.
I THINK HE'S PART OF THE PROBLEM.

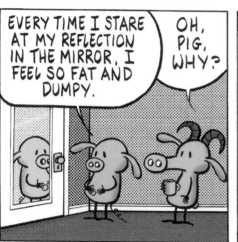

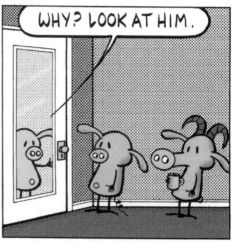

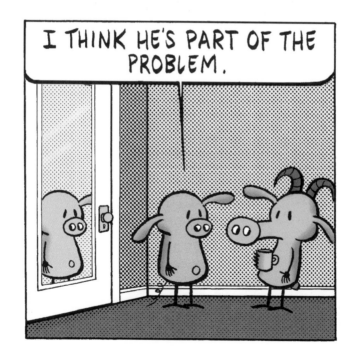

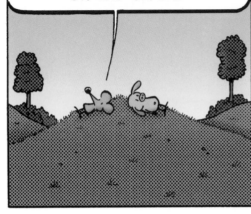

WHAT DO YOU DO WHEN SOMEONE MAKES YOU FEEL STRESSED OR SAD OR BAD?

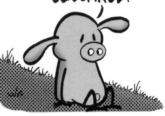

I PRETEND I'M A LITTLE KID AGAIN AND I'M SNEAKING THROUGH MY CHILDHOOD HOME. I TRY TO REMEMBER HOW DOORS OPENED, HOW CLOSETS SMELLED, HOW FLOORS SQUEAKED.

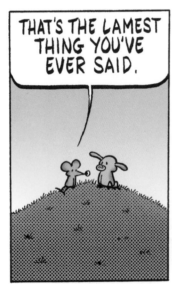

THAT'S THE LAMEST THING YOU'VE EVER SAID.

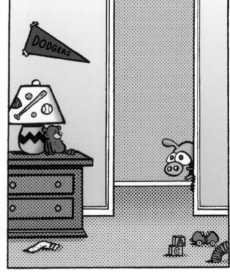

HEY, PIG...WHAT WOULD YOU THINK IF YOU AND I WERE BURIED TOGETHER ONE DAY? WE COULD SPLIT THE COST OF THE GRAVESITE AND ALL.
OH MY GOODNESS. I'D BE HONORED.
OH. GOOD, BECAUSE I ALREADY HAD IT BUILT.

RAT
He Made The Little People Laugh...
COMICS TRAIL-BLAZER
CAN WE PUT MY NAME SOMEWHERE?
OH. YEAH. I SPRAY-PAINTED IT HERE.
PIG TOO

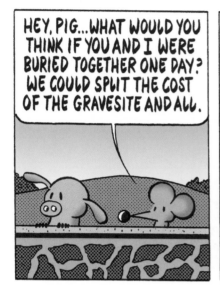

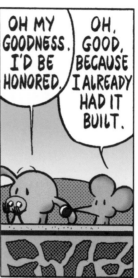

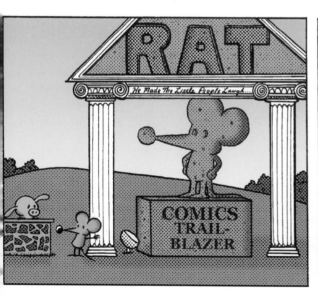

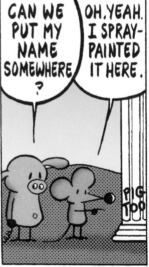

Hullo, son. Whuh you reading?
'THE SCARLET LETTER'...IT'S FOR MY ENGLISH CLASS. IT'S ABOUT A WOMAN LIVING IN THE SEVENTEENTH CENTURY WHO—
ZZZZZ
THUD
I THINK I MIGHT KNOW WHY YOU DIDN'T DO WELL IN ENGLISH, DAD.
Hey... how me get on floor?

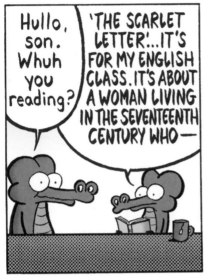

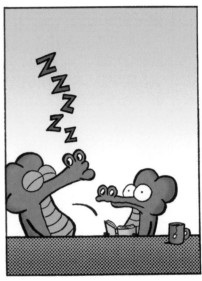

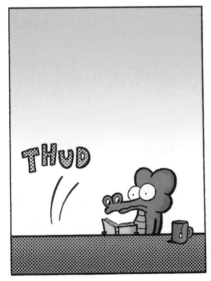

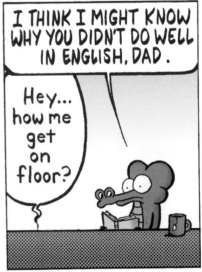

DO YOU THINK WE CAN LOOK TO THE STARS FOR DIRECTION AS TO WHAT WE SHOULD DO WITH OUR LIVES?
NO. WHY?
GIVE UP PIG
NO REASON.

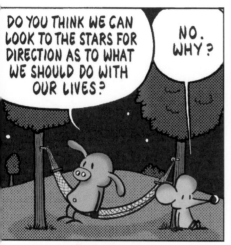

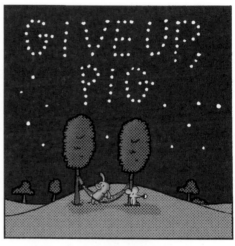

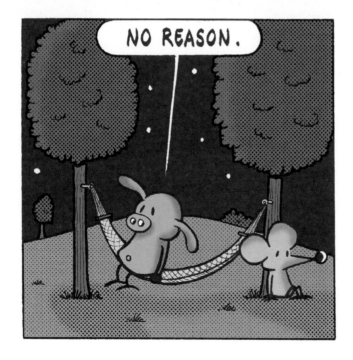

WHAT ARE YOU READING, GOAT?
THE COMPLETE WORKS OF ALEXANDER PUSHKIN.
OH, I *LOVE* THAT GUY.
YOU DO? HOW DO YOU KNOW HIM?
HE KEEPS ALL MY PAPERS STUCK TO THE BULLETIN BOARD.
THAT'S PUSH PIN.
OH. MAYBE THEY'RE BROTHERS.

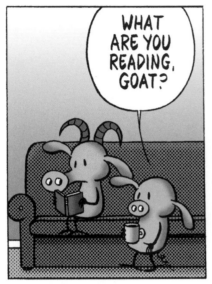

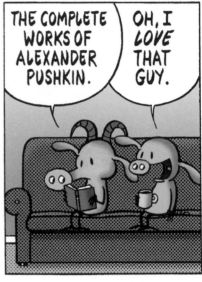

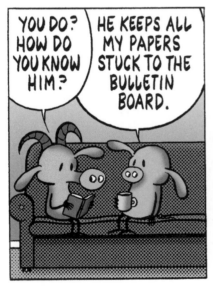

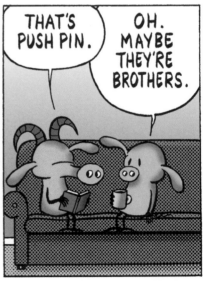

Hey, son... Want play Wii?
CAN'T. I HAVE TO WRITE A REPORT ON THE BOOK 'OF MICE AND MEN'.. WE HAVE TO COMPARE AND CONTRAST THE CHARACTERS.
Oh, peese. Dat like so easy.
HOW DO YOU FIGURE?
Mice is small. Men wear pants.
THANKS, DAD.
Okay.. Now you play Wii?

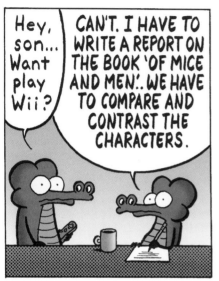

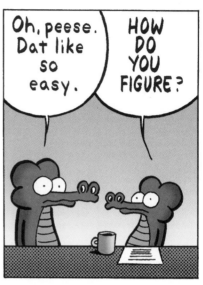

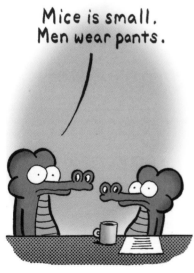

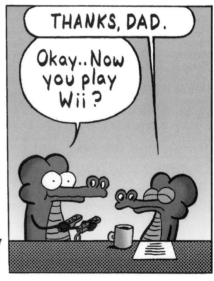

WHAT ARE YOU LOOKING AT, PIG?
I'M SEARCHING FOR MY YIAYIA.
WHAT'S A YIAYIA?
IT'S WHAT WE CALLED MY GRAND-MOTHER. SHE DIED WHEN I WAS FIVE. I KEEP HOPING I CAN FIND HER IN THE STARS.
PIG...DECEASED PEOPLE DO NOT BECOME CONSTELLATIONS.
THEY DO IN GREEK MYTHOLOGY.

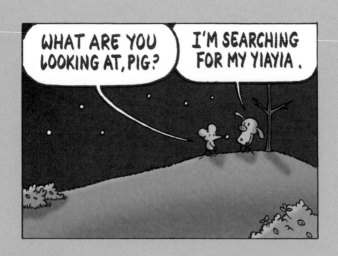

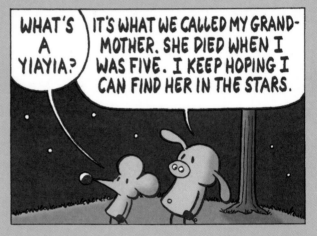

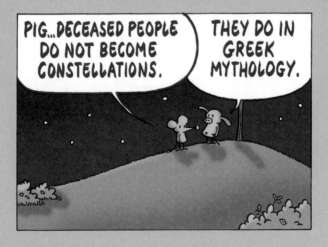

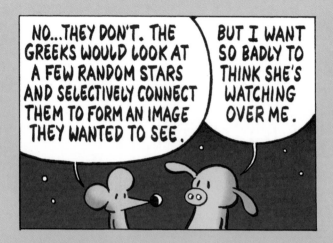

NO...THEY DON'T. THE GREEKS WOULD LOOK AT A FEW RANDOM STARS AND SELECTIVELY CONNECT THEM TO FORM AN IMAGE THEY WANTED TO SEE.

BUT I WANT SO BADLY TO THINK SHE'S WATCHING OVER ME.

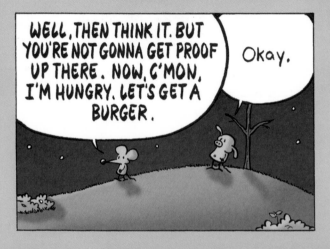

WELL, THEN THINK IT. BUT YOU'RE NOT GONNA GET PROOF UP THERE. NOW, C'MON, I'M HUNGRY. LET'S GET A BURGER.

Okay.

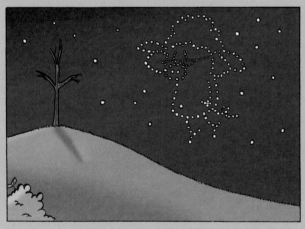

Hey, son, want play Wii?
I CAN'T. I HAVE TO GO TO A CLASSMATE'S HOUSE TO DISSECT A FROG FOR MY SCIENCE CLASS.. IT'LL PROBABLY TAKE ALL AFTERNOON.
Whuh 'dissect' mean?
YOU CUT IT UP. AND IT'S A PRETTY INVOLVED PROCESS, SO THERE'S NOT MUCH I CAN DO TO SPEED THINGS UP.
SCIENTISTS WORK A LITTLE SLOWER THAN THAT, DAD.
Dey must no have Wii.

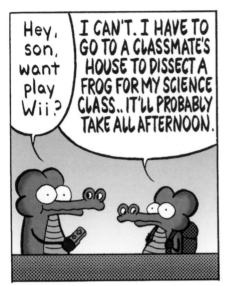

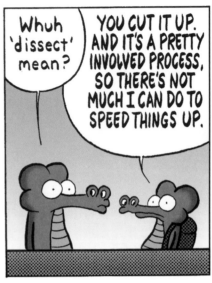

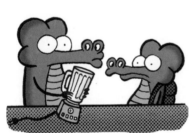

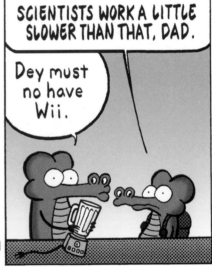

LOOK AT THIS...MY STUPID CONTRACTOR INSTALLED THE WRONG FRONT DOOR. THIS ONE'S GOT ONE OF THOSE MAIL SLOTS.
WHAT'S WRONG WITH THAT? I LIKE BEING ABLE TO GET MY MAIL DROPPED RIGHT INTO MY HOUSE.

I DON'T.
Hey. Tell heem you Fed Ex guy.
Hi. Me Fed Ex guy.

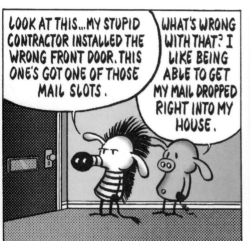

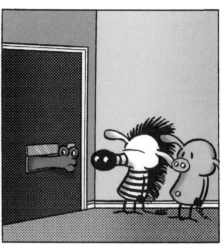

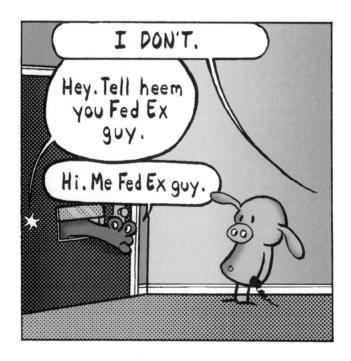

BYE, MOM.
HAVE A GOOD DAY AT SCHOOL, SWEETIE...STUDY HARD.
SPROINNNG
YOU KNOW, DAD, SOME FATHERS *LIKE* THEIR KID TO ATTEND SCHOOL.
Not me. Stay home. Play Wii.
HEY, SUPER MARIO, LOOK OVER HERE.

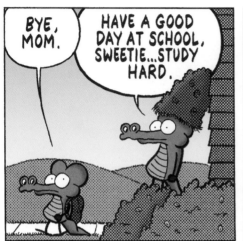

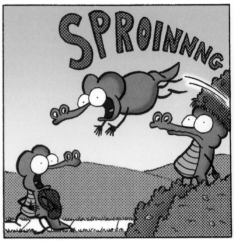

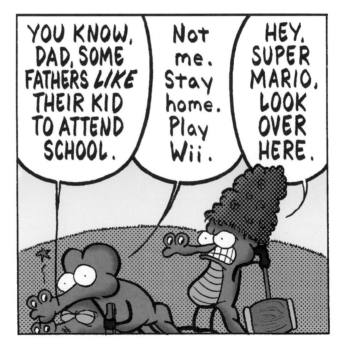

WHAT ARE YOU DOING?
STARING AT THIS ANT AND WONDERING.
WONDERING WHAT?
IF HE HAS ALL THE DAILY STRUGGLES AND WORRIES THAT WE DO. AND IF SO, WHAT I COULD DO TO HELP HIM GET RID OF THEM.
SQOOOSH
THERE'S THAT.

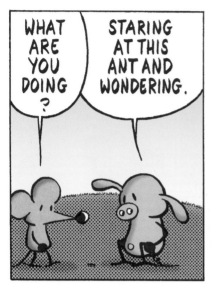

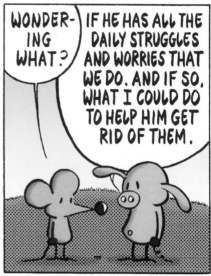

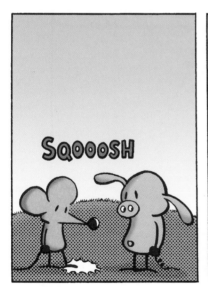

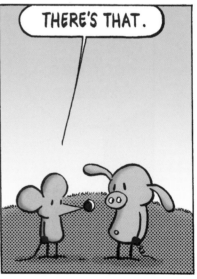

TONIGHT ON 'NATIONAL GEOGRAPHIC,' WE EXPLORE THE WORLD OF AFRICAN PREDATORS AND THEIR PREY. SO COME....
... JOIN US.
THEY DON'T MEAN IT LITERALLY, DAD.
Whoa. Ees dark een Afreeca.

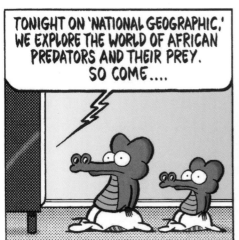

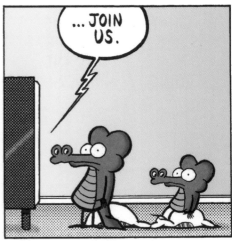

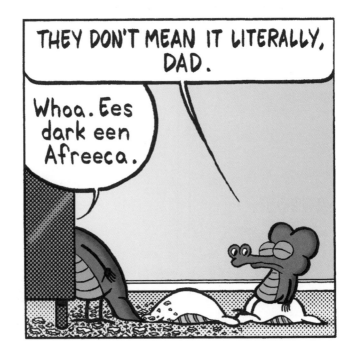

MY ETHICAL CONDUCT HAS BEGUN TO SINK BELOW EVEN MY STANDARDS. I THINK IT'S TIME FOR ME TO CHANGE.
I'M SURPRISED TO HEAR YOU SAY THAT, RAT. WHAT ARE YOU GOING TO DO?
LOWER MY ETHICAL STANDARDS.
SOME PEOPLE MIGHT CHANGE THEIR CONDUCT.
WHY TAKE THE HARD ROAD?

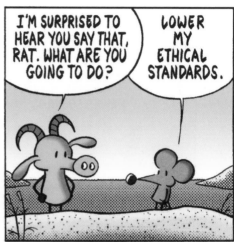

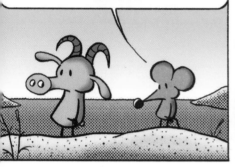

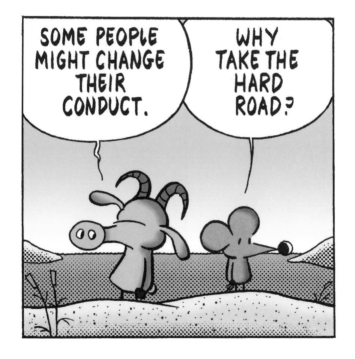

WHAT'S THE MATTER WITH YOU, RAT?
I'M STRUGGLING TO FIGURE OUT WHY IT IS THAT SOME PEOPLE SUCCEED AT EVERY-THING THEY DO...IT RAISES SO MANY QUESTIONS.
LIKE WHAT? MAYBE I CAN HELP.
WELL...LIKE... WHAT DO THEY HAVE THAT THE REST OF US DON'T?
SUCCESS.
I CAN BE A TERRIFIC RESOURCE.

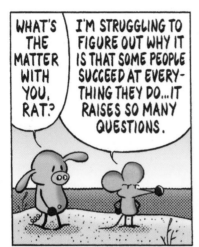

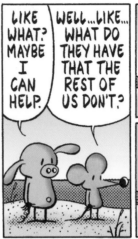

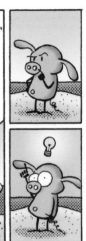

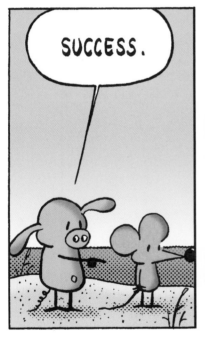

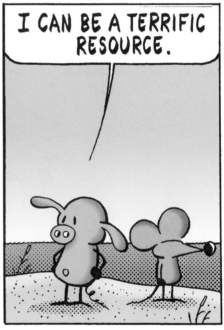

WHAT ARE YOU DOING, PIG?
I'VE STARTED STUDYING ROCKS. THIS IS MY COLLECTION.
HEY, THAT'S GREAT! NOW IF I REMEMBER CORRECTLY, THERE ARE THREE KINDS OF ROCK, RIGHT? IGNEOUS, SEDIMENTARY AND METAMORPHIC? SO WHAT DO YOU CALL THAT ONE IN YOUR HANDS?
THE BUMPY ONE.

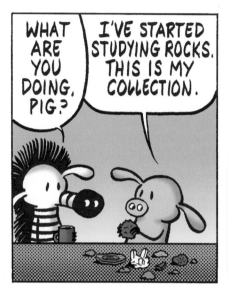

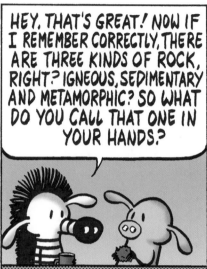

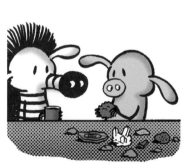

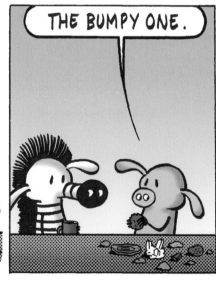

TWO FRIED EGGS.
THANK YOU.

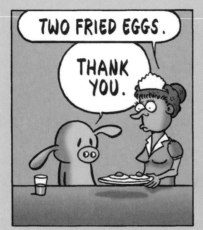

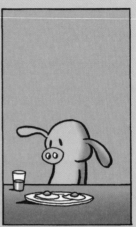

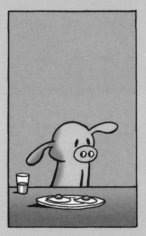

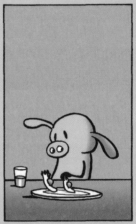

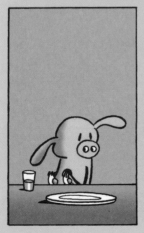

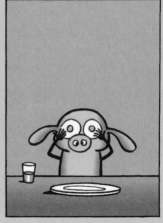

POKE POKE
I'D LIKE TO BE SEATED SOMEWHERE ELSE.
THE FAT PIG STARTED IT.
HEY, I DON'T POKE YOU IN THE FRIED EGG EYES.

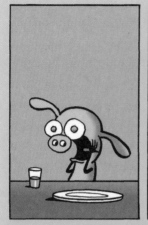

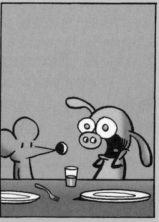

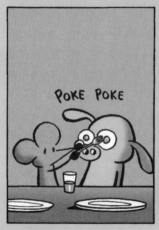

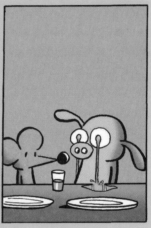

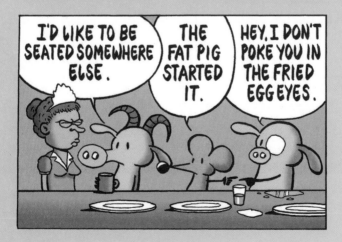

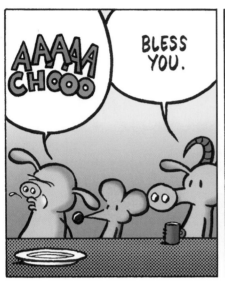

AAAAA CHOOO

BLESS YOU.

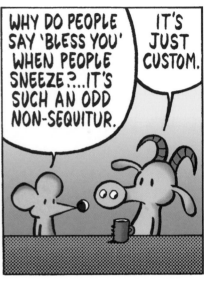

WHY DO PEOPLE SAY 'BLESS YOU' WHEN PEOPLE SNEEZE?...IT'S SUCH AN ODD NON-SEQUITUR.

IT'S JUST CUSTOM.

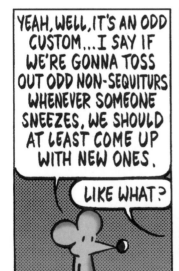

YEAH, WELL, IT'S AN ODD CUSTOM....I SAY IF WE'RE GONNA TOSS OUT ODD NON-SEQUITURS WHENEVER SOMEONE SNEEZES, WE SHOULD AT LEAST COME UP WITH NEW ONES.

LIKE WHAT?

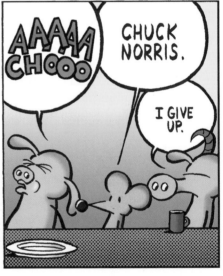

AAAAA CHOOO

CHUCK NORRIS.

I GIVE UP.

DUDE...WHY IS THIS GROCERY BAG FILLED WITH FORTY BOTTLES OF HAIR GEL?
I BOUGHT THEM.
YOU HAVE NO HAIR.
I'M A SUCKER FOR A SALE.

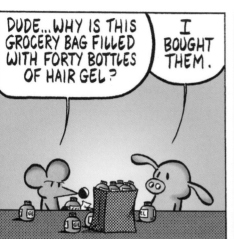

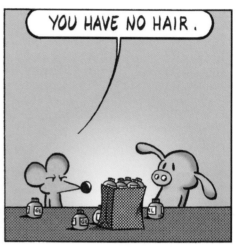

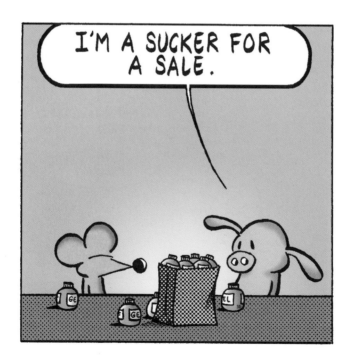

I HEARD YOU AND PIG HAD A SÉANCE TO CONJURE UP THE SOULS OF FAMOUS GUYS WHO DIED TRAGICALLY.
YEAH, AND THE ONLY GUY PIG COULD THINK OF WAS HUMPTY DUMPTY.
YOU KNOW, SOME PEOPLE THINK YOU SHOULDN'T MESS WITH THAT STUFF BECAUSE THE SOUL CAN BE PERMANENTLY DRAWN TO THE ENERGY OF YOUR HOME.
WHAT THE HECK DOES THAT MEAN?
... AND REALLY, WHAT KIND OF KING SENDS HORSES TO REPAIR EGGS?
CAN I GO TO SLEEP NOW, HUMPTY?

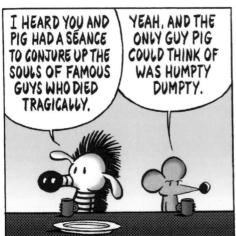

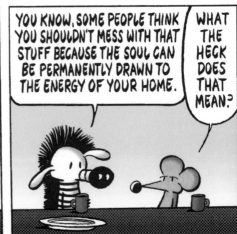

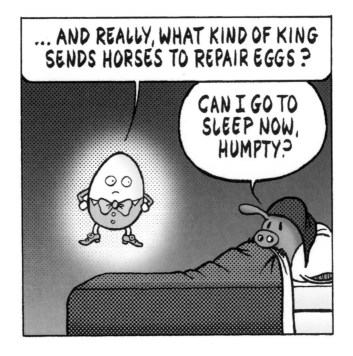

HI. HOW MUCH FOR A CUP OF COFFEE?
TWO BUCKS. BUT YOU CAN GET AS MANY REFILLS AS YOU WANT. IT'S BOTTOMLESS.
OH, GREAT... THEN ONE COFFEE, PLEASE.
MORE PLEASE.

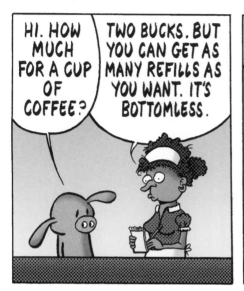

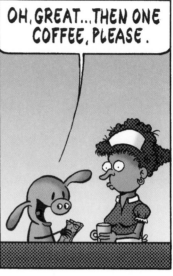

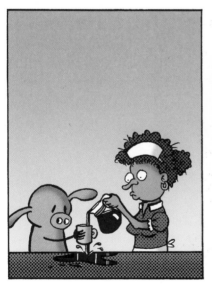

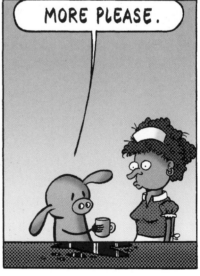

HOW COME WE NEVER GO IN THE BASEMENT?
BECAUSE IT'S DARK AND WE DON'T KNOW WHAT'S IN THERE.
THAT'S STUPID. I'M GOING IN.
I THINK I KNOW WHY OUR AIR-CONDITIONING BILL IS SO HIGH.

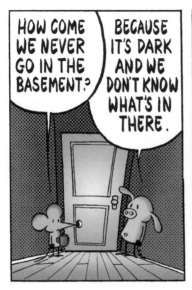

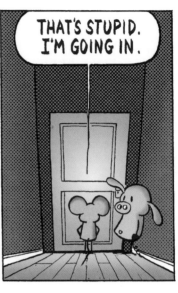

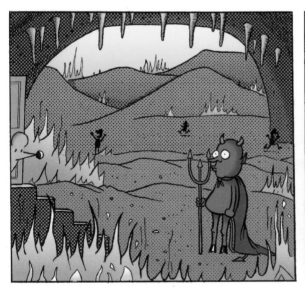

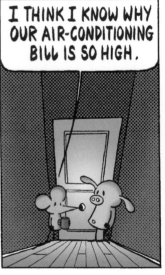

WHAT'S YOUR LIFE'S DREAM, PIG?
TO BE A MEMBER OF THE 'PINK AVENGERS,' AN ELITE CORPS OF FLYING PIGS WHO SWOOP DOWN FROM THE CLOUDS WHENEVER THEIR HOTLINE ALERTS THEM TO SOMEONE WHO IS CRUSHING THE ASPIRATIONS OF A PIG.
HOW STUPID.

RIIIIIIING

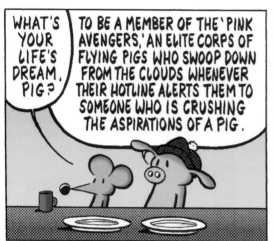

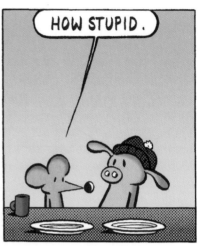

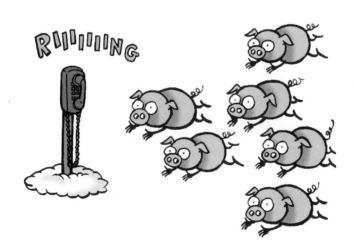

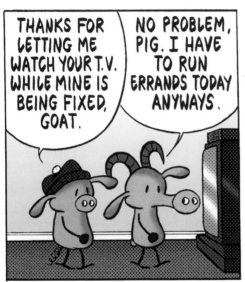

THANKS FOR LETTING ME WATCH YOUR T.V. WHILE MINE IS BEING FIXED, GOAT.

NO PROBLEM, PIG. I HAVE TO RUN ERRANDS TODAY ANYWAYS.

ALRIGHT, SO THIS REMOTE TURNS THE T.V. ON AND OFF. THIS ONE'S FOR THE VOLUME. THIS ONE'S FOR THE CABLE BOX. THIS ONE'S FOR THE STEREO RECEIVER. AND THIS ONE'S FOR THE DVD PLAYER. ANYHOW, HAVE FUN.

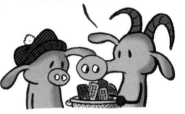

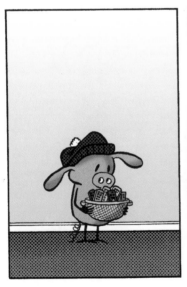

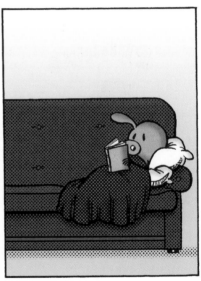

HEY THERE, PIG, WHATCHA DOIN'?
I'VE DECIDED THAT THE INTERNET IS A BAD PLACE. EVERYBODY'S MEAN. SO I'VE CREATED MY 'INTERNET HAPPY BOX.'
Internet Happy Box
WHAT DOES IT DO?
WELL, IT'S JUST LIKE THE INTERNET, ONLY IT'S NOT HOOKED UP TO ANYTHING AND YOU CAN'T COMMUNICATE WITH ANYONE AND IT'S DARK.
Internet Happy Box

I DON'T THINK THAT'S REALLY LIKE THE INTERNET, PIG.
WAIT 'TIL I POST ABOUT *THIS* ON THE MESSAGE BOARDS.
INTERNET HAPPY BOX! INTERNET HAPPY BOX!
Internet Happy Box

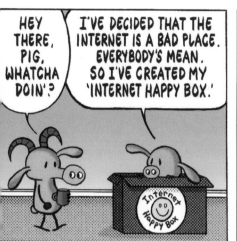

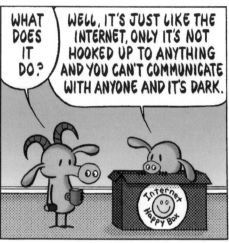

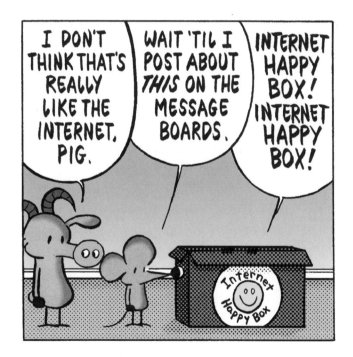

WHAT ARE YOU DOING, RAT?
I'M STANDING BEHIND THE COOL FENCE.
COOL
THAT IS SO JUVENILE... THERE IS NO SUCH THING AS A 'COOL FENCE' AND AN 'UNCOOL FENCE.'
COOL
YES, THERE IS. I'M BEHIND IT.
Uncool
PIG, YOU DON'T HAVE TO ACCEPT HIS CLASSIFICATION.
BUT IT'S TRUE.
Uncool
NO! DON'T YOU GET IT, PIG? RAT DOES THIS BECAUSE HE'S INSECURE. DON'T BUY INTO THAT!
BUT I'M NOT COOL.

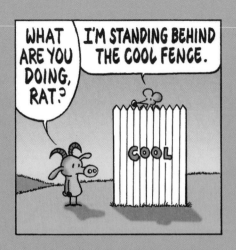

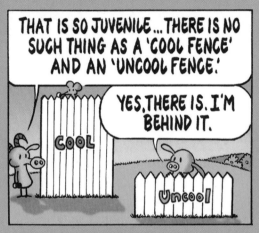

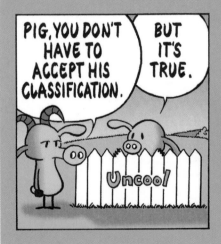

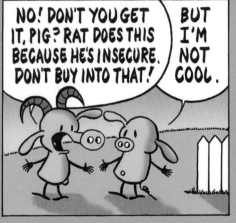

YES YOU ARE!
NO, I'M NOT!
YES YOU ARE!!
NO, I'M NOT!!
STOP FIGHTING, NERDS!
COOL
SEE?
I'M GONNA CLIMB THAT FENCE AND—
HEY HEY HEY... DON'T YOU NERDIFY MY FENCE.
COOL

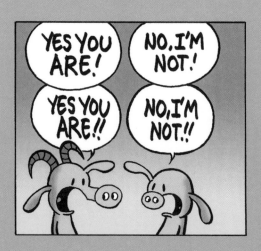

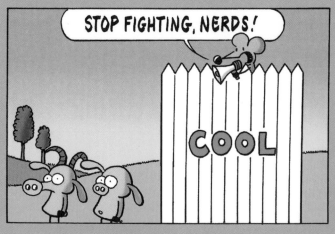

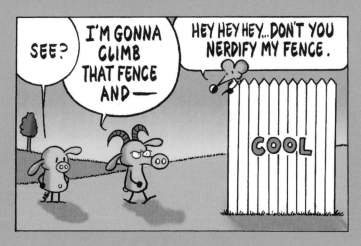

HEY THERE, PIG.. WHY YOU WEARING A MASK?
RAT MADE ME.
WHAT FOR?
HE SAYS STUPIDITY CAN BE CONTAGIOUS.
IT'S A GLOBAL EPIDEMIC.

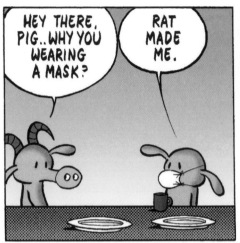

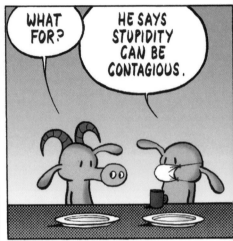

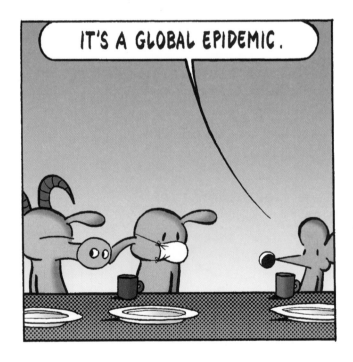

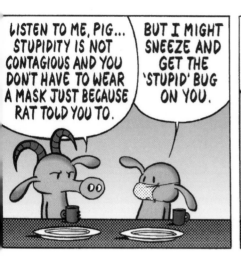

LISTEN TO ME, PIG... STUPIDITY IS NOT CONTAGIOUS AND YOU DON'T HAVE TO WEAR A MASK JUST BECAUSE RAT TOLD YOU TO.

BUT I MIGHT SNEEZE AND GET THE 'STUPID' BUG ON YOU.

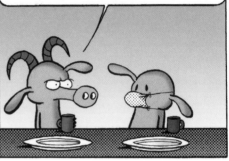

PIG...YOU ARE NOT STUPID. YOU ARE ENTITLED TO DIGNITY AND RESPECT, AS IS EVERY LIVING BEING ON THIS EARTH.

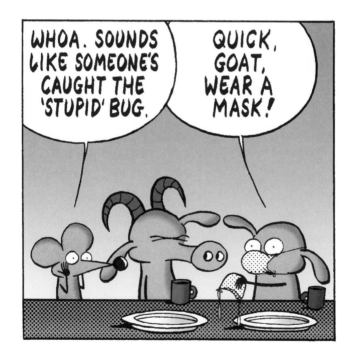

WHOA. SOUNDS LIKE SOMEONE'S CAUGHT THE 'STUPID' BUG.

QUICK, GOAT, WEAR A MASK!

WHAT ARE YOU DOING, PIG?
I THREW A MESSAGE-IN-A-BOTTLE IN THE WATER. I'M HOPING IT REACHES SOME FAR-OFF CIVILIZATION, WHO'LL SEND ME A MESSAGE BACK.
MAYBE THE RING AROUND THE TUB WILL CONTACT YOU.
WHERE'S A CURRENT WHEN YOU NEED ONE?

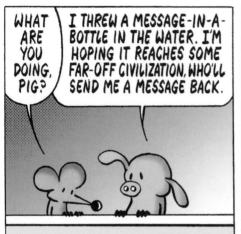

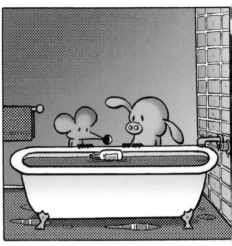

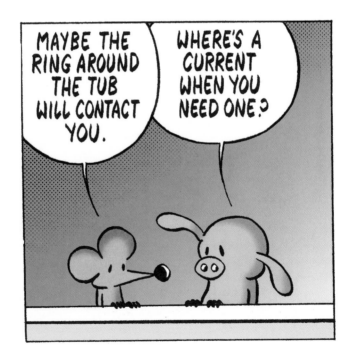

WHAT DO YOU THINK YOU'RE DOING?
I'VE WRITTEN A BOOK AND I'M HERE SIGNING COPIES... COME, CELEBRATE THE ACCOMPLISHMENTS OF A FRIEND AND GET YOUR OWN SIGNED COPY.
AUTHOR BOOK SIGNING 2 pm - 4 pm
KILLING ZEEBAS FOR DUMMIES
A Step-by-Step Guide
AUTHOR BOOK SIGNING 2 pm - 4 pm
YOU'RE REALLY HOLDING UP THE LINE.
FOR DUMMIES
A Step-by-Step Guide
AUTHOR BOOK SIGNING 2 pm - 4 pm

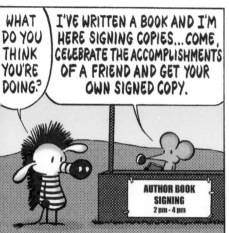

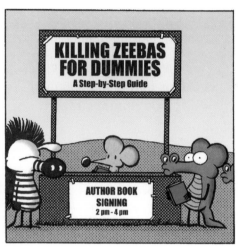

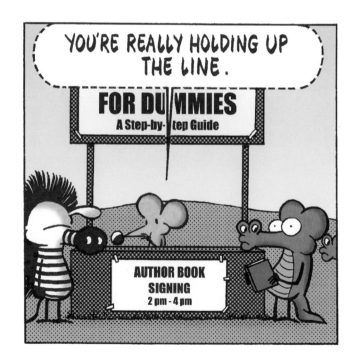

RAT'S 'KILLING ZEEBAS FOR DUMMIES' BOOK

One way to intimidate your enemy is to learn and exploit one of his childhood fears.

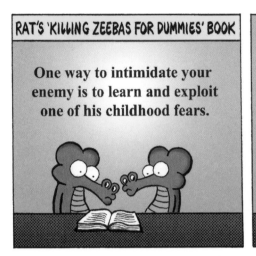

For some, that fear is born of a childhood dog bite. For others, a neighborhood bully. And for still others, a bad experience at the circus.

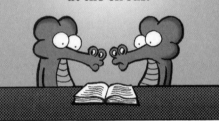

FOR THE LAST TIME, I AM NOT AFRAID OF 'GIANT CLOWN HEAD.'

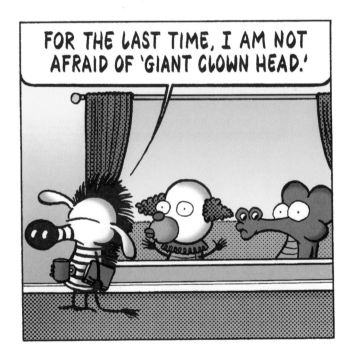

WHAT HAPPENED TO YOU?
I WAS DRIVING DOWNTOWN AND I HIT A PARKED CAR.
OHMYGAWD.. DID YOU LEAVE A NOTE ON THEIR WINDSHIELD?
OF COURSE I LEFT A NOTE ON THEIR WINDSHIELD.
WHAT'D IT SAY?
IT SAID, 'DUDE, YOUR CAR IS MESSED UP.'
SOME PEOPLE LEAVE PHONE NUMBERS.
I PREFER TO SHOW EMPATHY.

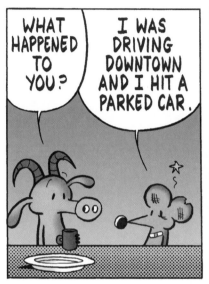

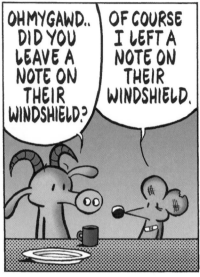

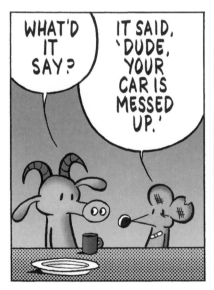

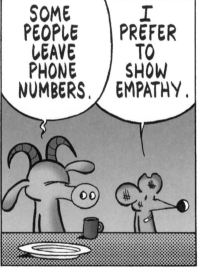

THERE'S A GUY AT THE DOOR FROM THE PARKS DEPARTMENT. HE WANTS TO KNOW IF THERE ARE ANY POOR SWIMMERS HERE IN NEED OF SWIMMING LESSONS.
TELL HIM NO. WE KNOW HOW TO SWIM.
NO.
HE SEEMED DISAPPOINTED.

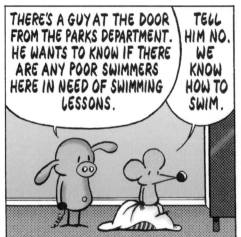

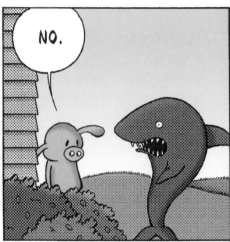

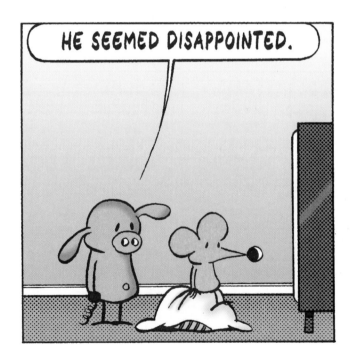

HEY, ZEBRA, I THINK I JUST HEARD A NOISE FROM UNDER YOUR FLOOR.
IT'S THE CROCS. THEY'VE DISCOVERED THE CRAWL SPACE. THEY'RE TRYING TO USE IT TO GET INTO THE HOUSE.
HOW DO YOU KNOW IT'S THEM?
BECAUSE EVERY TIME THEY SMASH THEIR SNOUTS ON THE FLOOR JOISTS, THEY TRY TO DISGUISE WHO THEY ARE.
THUD

Whoa. Me is one huge ant.
OH.
Hey... My snout really hurt, Floyd.
Shut mouf, Bob. We is *ants*.

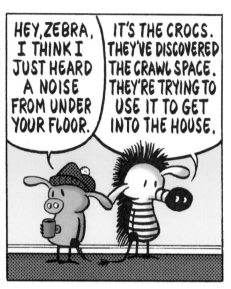

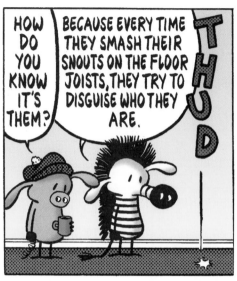

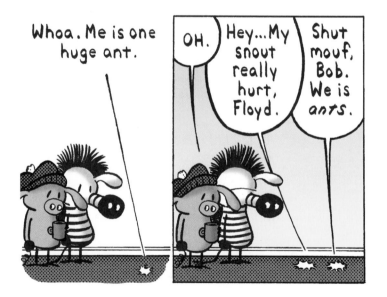

WHAT ARE YOU DOING NOW, LARRY?
Me ees writing een diary Bob buy for me at grocery store. Me get idea from 'assassin log' me see on TV spy show.
WHAT ARE YOU TALKING ABOUT?

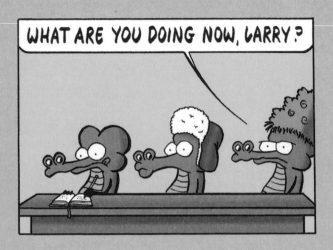

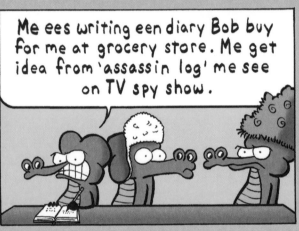

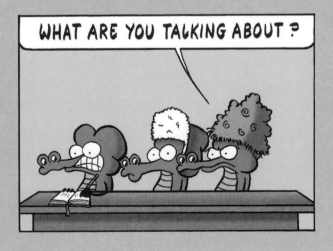

Me ees ASSASSIN, woomun. Me keep log of who me ees gonna KEEL, HOW me ees gonna keel, and how me ees gonna EET dem.
THAT WOULD PROBABLY BE MORE MENACING IF YOU DIDN'T HAVE 'HELLO KITTY' PRINTED ON EVERY PAGE.
Me told you no to buy dis one.
Is only one store have.
OH, NO... IS THAT YOUR FIERCE 'HELLO KITTY' FACE?

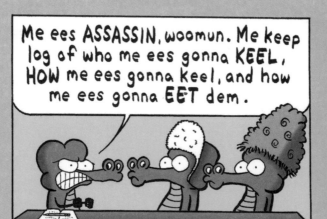

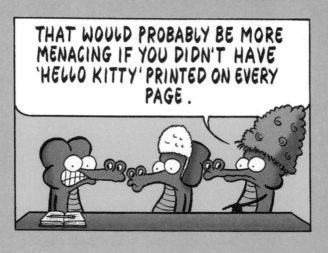

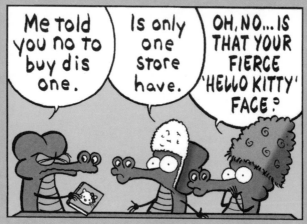

WHAT ARE YOU DOING, PIG?
BEING POPULAR.
WHAT MAKES YOU THINK YOU'RE POPULAR?
I'M SITTING IN THE POPULAR TREE.
IT'S CALLED A POPLAR TREE.
MIND HELPING ME DOWN SO I DON'T GET A BOO-BOO?

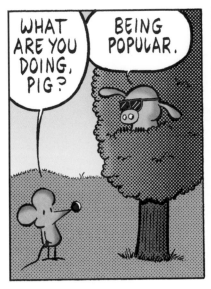

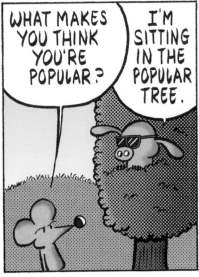

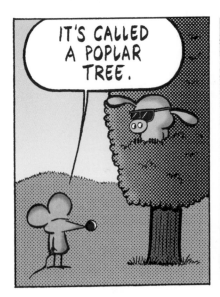

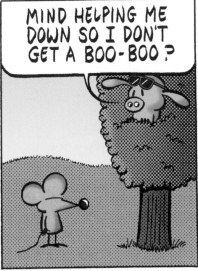

WHAT ARE YOU DOING, PIG?
EXERCISING.
YOU'RE NOT MOVING.
THAT'S WHAT I THOUGHT, BUT IT TURNS OUT THE WORLD IS ROTATING TO THE EAST, AND I HAVEN'T SLID BACK TOWARD THE COFFEE TABLE, SO I *MUST* BE MOVING.
I THINK I KNOW WHY YOU'RE NOT LOSING WEIGHT.
HANG ON. I'VE EARNED ANOTHER DONUT BREAK.

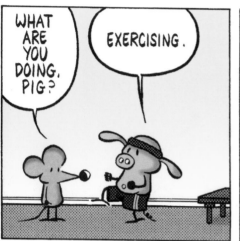

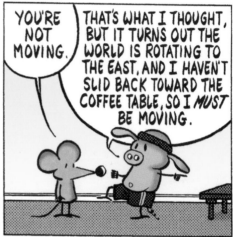

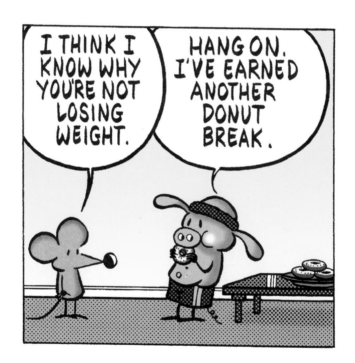

WHAT DO YOU GOT THERE?
KIKO, THE LONELY CACTUS. HE'S SAD BECAUSE NO ONE WILL HUG HIM.
OF COURSE THEY WON'T HUG HIM. HE'S GOT BIG, SHARP SPIKES THAT WILL STAB WHOEVER HE TOUCHES.
I TOLD YOU PERSONALITY COUNTS FOR NOTHING.

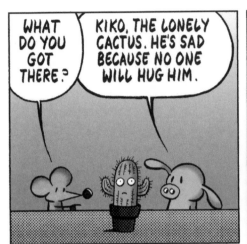

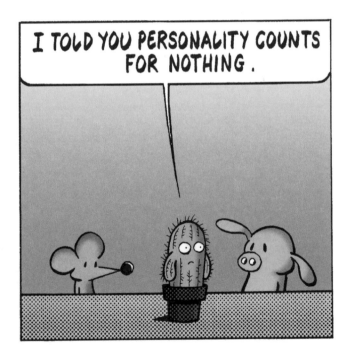

KIKO, THE LONELY CACTUS
YOU KNOW, KIKO, NOT ONLY DOES NO ONE WANT TO HUG A CACTUS, BUT NO ONE WANTS TO BE WITH SOMEONE WHO PROJECTS NEED. DO YOU THINK THAT'S PART OF YOUR PROBLEM?
HUG ME!!
NO.
POP

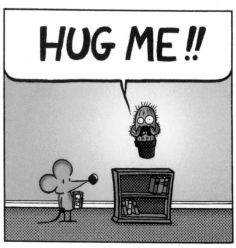

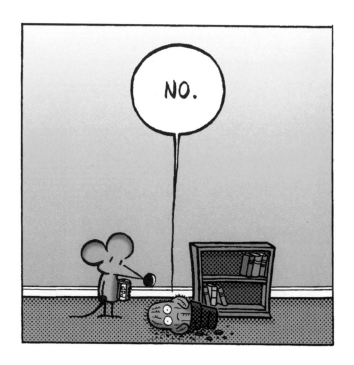

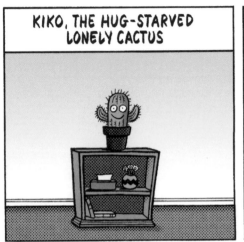

KIKO, THE HUG-STARVED
LONELY CACTUS

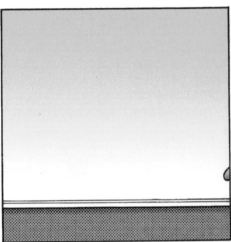

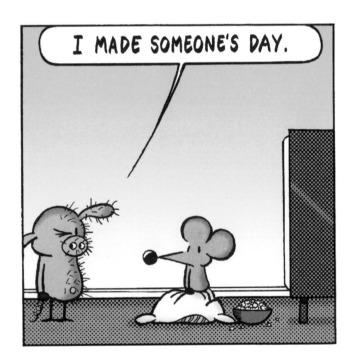

I MADE SOMEONE'S DAY.

DID THE WRITERS OF THE U.S. CONSTITUTION HAVE TO MAKE IT MORE APPEALING TO RATS BEFORE THE STATES WOULD AGREE TO IT?
NO.
SO THEY DIDN'T HAVE TO ADD IN SPECIAL PROVISIONS THAT ONLY RATS WANTED?
NO.
THAT IS NOT WHAT RATIFY MEANS.
OH? THEN WHY WASN'T IT PIGIFIED?

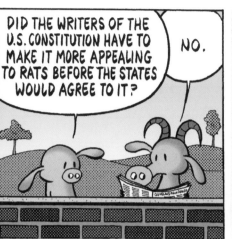

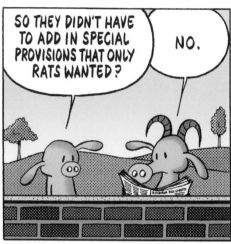

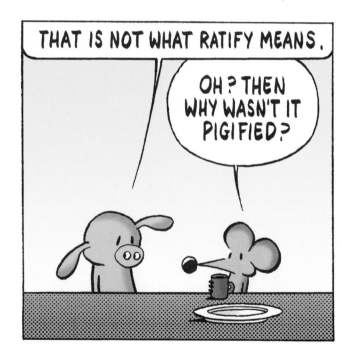

WHAT ARE YOU DOING, PIG?
I'M STANDING BEHIND THE UNCOOL FENCE.
Uncool
THE UNCOOL FENCE?? WHAT THE?... WHY??
BECAUSE THE COOL PEOPLE DON'T WANT ME BEHIND THEIR FENCE.
WHO TOLD YOU THAT?
Uncool
GREETINGS, NERD.
COOL
Uncool

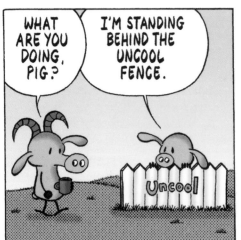

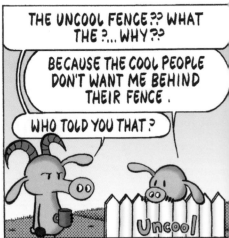

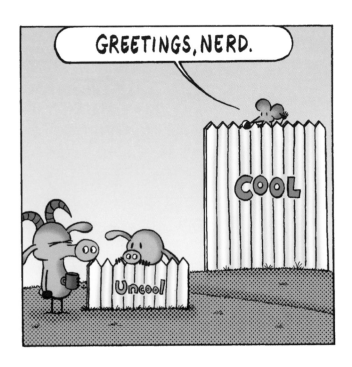

Hulloooo, zeeba neighba...Leesten. Mebbe you hear crocs catch zeeba last week.
DON'T TALK TO ME. THAT WAS MY COUSIN NICKY. AND YOU KNOW THAT.
Well, leesten...Mebbe you help us eemprove by filling out customer sateesfaction form. See, it ask, 'Was crocs courteous during keeling?'...'Was we punctual?'...'Deed we eet you frend een professional manner?' Oh, and juss for parteecipating een survey, you geet special prize!
Mebbe zeeba meat not gud special prize.

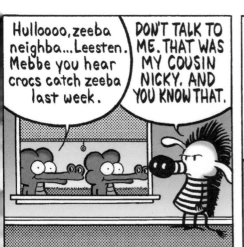

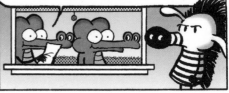

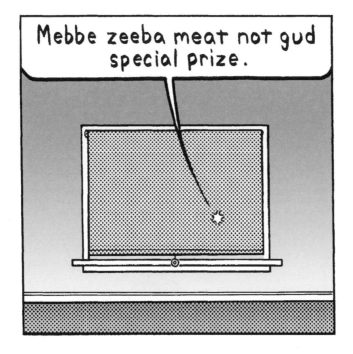

Assassin Log:
DAY ONE
Tooday me see TV nayture show abowt crocs.
Me see one croc who lurk all day een shallow swamp and wait for zeeba arive.
Zeeba finaly arive. He no expekk nutteeng. Croc pop out of reeds. Croc snap zeeba nekk.

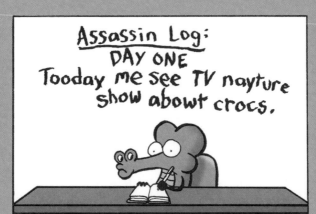

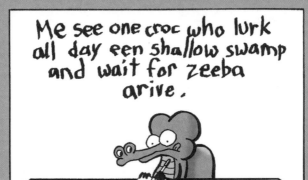

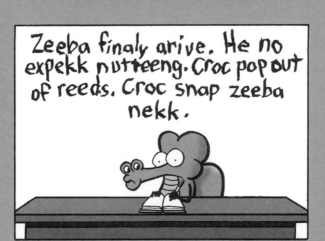

Tooday me try exakk same ting.
GET OUT OF MY POOL, LARRY.
T.V. beeg fat lie.

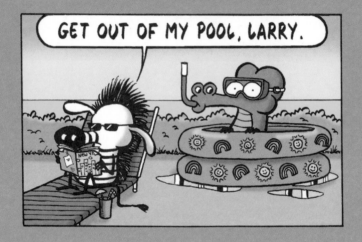

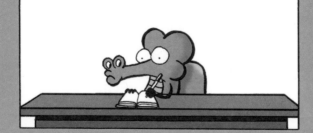

HEY, GOAT, WANNA COME TO MY PARTY? I FIGURE IF WE'RE ALL GONNA BE LABELED 'UNCOOL,' WE CAN AT LEAST COME TOGETHER FOR SOME GOOD MUSIC AND MUNCHIES.
WELL, NOW *THAT'S* THE SPIRIT, PIG! WE CAN HAVE A *GREAT* TIME TOGETHER!
Uncool
SODA
CALL IT NERDAPALOOZA!
COOL
I'M GONNA KILL HIM.
HEY, IT DOES MAKE A NICE SHIRT.
Uncool
Nerda-Palooza

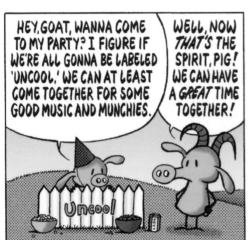

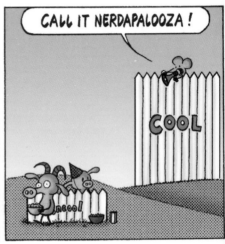

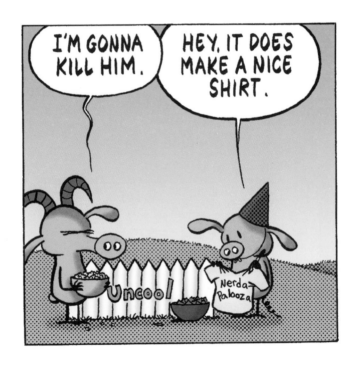

I'VE CONCLUDED THAT THE WORLD WOULD BE A MUCH BETTER PLACE IF WE'D ALL BE A LITTLE LESS SELFISH AND JUST START TREATING EACH OTHER BETTER.
GOOD FOR YOU, RAT... SO WHAT ARE YOU GONNA DO ABOUT IT?
WAIT FOR THE WORLD TO START TREATING ME BETTER.
OF COURSE.
I'M OWED, BABY... I'M OWED!

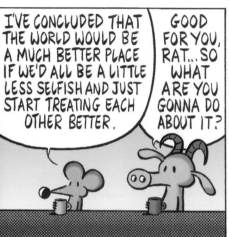

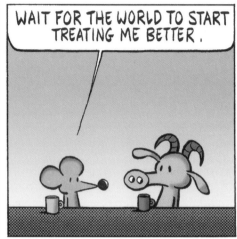

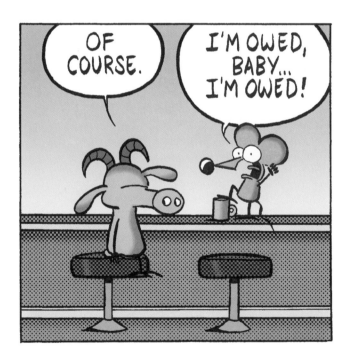

WHAT ARE YOU DOING, PIG?
I'M WISHING ON A SUPERNOVA.
A SUPER-NOVA? THAT'S A STAR THAT'S COLLAPSING IN ON ITSELF.
I KNOW. RAT SAID I SHOULD WISH ON IT BECAUSE THAT WAY WHEN MY DREAMS IMPLODE IT WILL ALL MAKE COSMIC SENSE.
WHY YOU LITTLE...
LOOK, PIG, A BLACK HOLE... THROW YOUR HOPES DOWN IT.

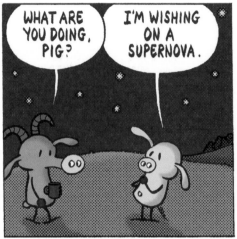

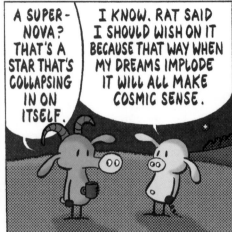

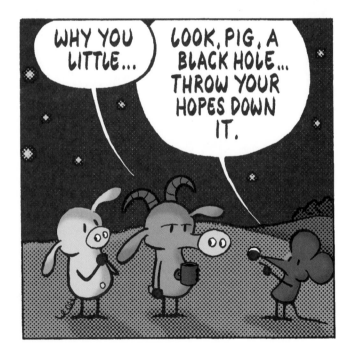

WHAT ARE YOU DOING, PIG?
I AM MONKEYPIG.
WHY?
BECAUSE I'M LONELY AND I CAN'T FIND LOVE. AND WHEN YOU'RE LONELY AND CAN'T FIND LOVE, YOU MIGHT AS WELL BE MONKEYPIG.
I'M JUST SUPPORTING A FRIEND.

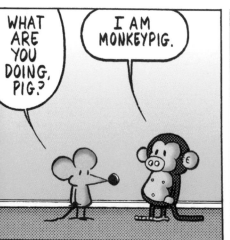

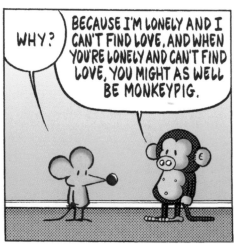

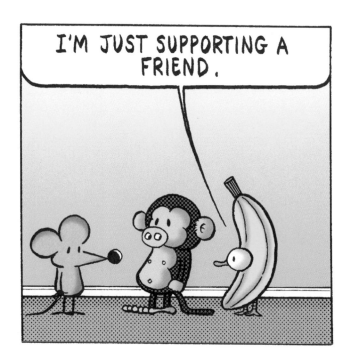

WHAT ARE YOU DOING, PIG?
SELF-AFFIRMATION.. YOU STARE AT YOUR REFLECTION IN THE MIRROR AND SAY GOOD THINGS...'YOU ARE LOVED, PIG...YOU ARE LOVED, PIG... YOU ARE LOVED, PIG.'
I FIND THAT HARD TO BELIEVE.
I WISH HE'D STOP DOING THAT.

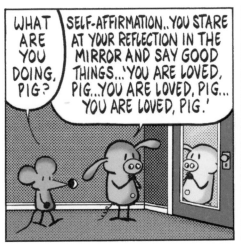

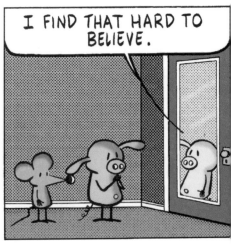

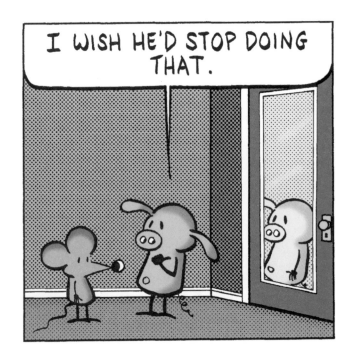

HEY, GOAT... WHERE WERE YOU YESTERDAY?
I WENT TO THE PARK. IT WAS SO BEAUTIFUL. THE SUN WAS JUST SETTING AS I GOT THERE AND IT WAS REFLECTING OFF THE LAKE. SOMETIMES THAT PLACE IS—
UH UH UH UH UH UH
WHAT?
YOU'VE REACHED 140 CHARACTERS.
THIS IS NOT 'TWITTER.'
PIPE DOWN. YOU'VE BEEN TWITTIFIED.

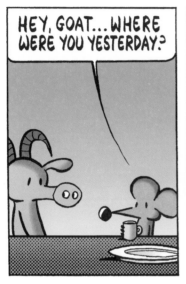

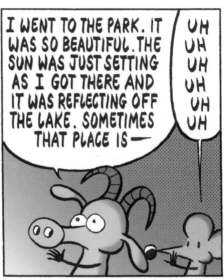

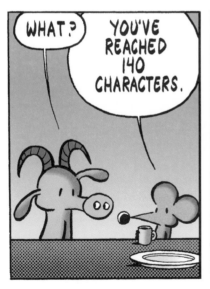

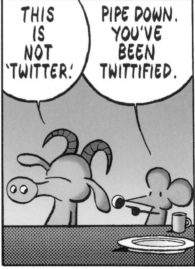

HI, ZEBRA. IT'S ME, PIG.
HI, PIG. WHAT'S UP?
WELL.... ARE YOU SITTING DOWN?
OH, MY GOD... NO. WHY?
BECAUSE I AM. AND IT'S SO DARN COMFY.
PLEASE DON'T START YOUR CONVERSATIONS THAT WAY.
WHAT DO YOU HAVE AGAINST COMFY?
CHEESE POOFS

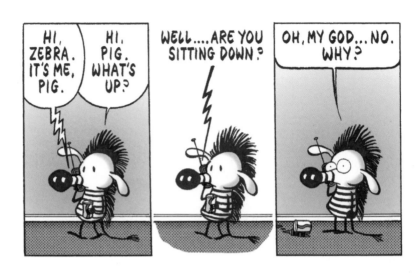

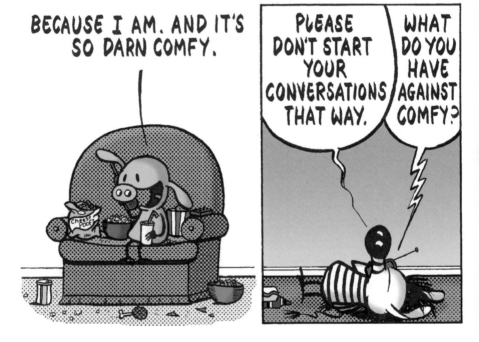

HEY THERE, GOAT... WHATCHA BEEN DOING LATELY?
I'VE BEEN TRYING TO BUILD A SHIP IN A BOTTLE. IT'S VERY HARD.
I IMAGINE. YOUR HEAD IS HUGE.
I DON'T GET INSIDE THE BOTTLE.
HEY, WANT TO SEE MY FRIEND SHOVE HIMSELF IN YOUR COKE?
NO.

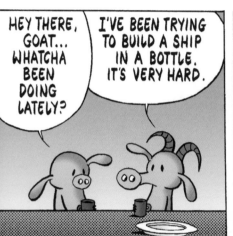

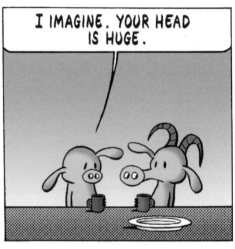

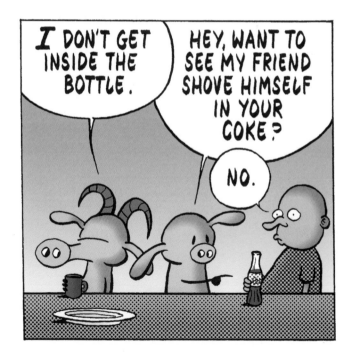

HEY DAD... WHY YOU HIDING BEHIND THE CURTAIN?
Zeeba neighba has new ally. Super smart guy. Lives in zeeba house. Zeeba turn to heem for answer to everyting.
SO YOU'RE HIDING FROM HIM?
Of course me hiding. Leesten, son... When guy dat smart, you not know what he do.

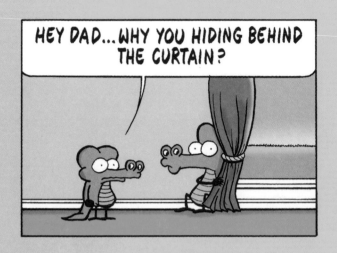

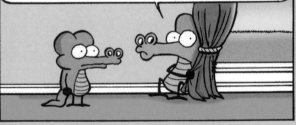

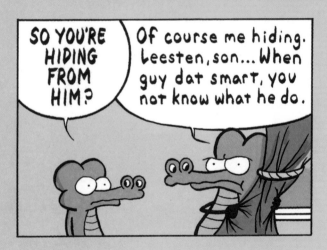

DID ZEBRA SAY HIS NAME?
Da GOOGLE.
DAD COULD USE A COMPUTER CLASS.
YOU NO TAKE ME ALIVE, DA GOOGLE!!

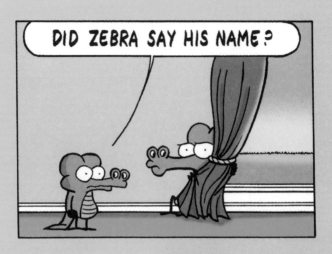

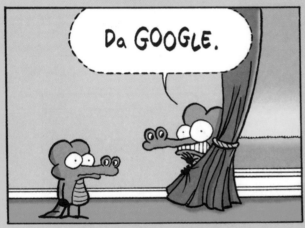

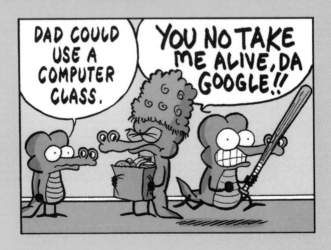

THIS BIOGRAPHY OF MARCO POLO IS THE GREATEST... DO YOU KNOW WHO MARCO POLO IS, PIG?
DO I? YOU BET I DO.
WHO?
HE INVENTED THE SWIMMING POOL.

NO.
MARCO
POLO

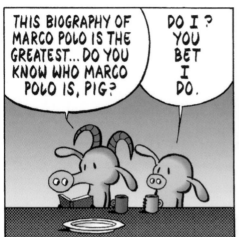

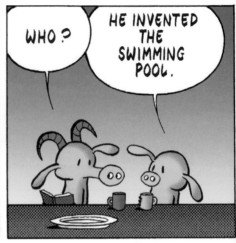

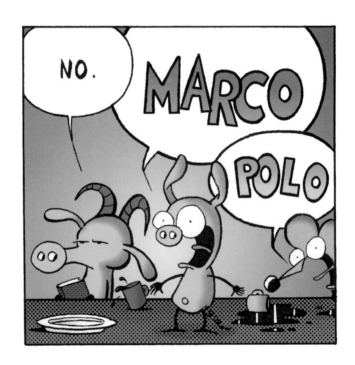

WHAT ARE YOU DOING, RAT?
SPRAYING THIS POLISH ON OUR TABLES. THE LABEL SAYS IT RESTORES STUFF TO ITS 'ORIGINAL LUSTER.' I'M DONE IF YOU WANT TO USE IT.
PSSHHHHHHHHHH
SIGH.

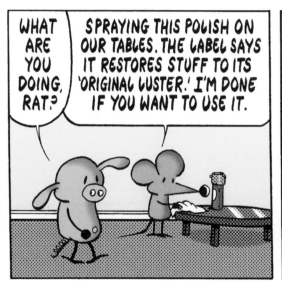

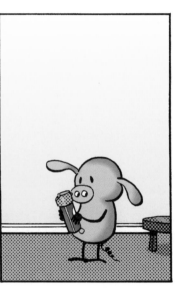

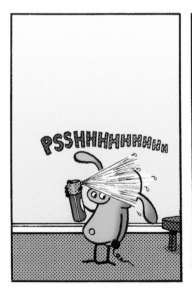

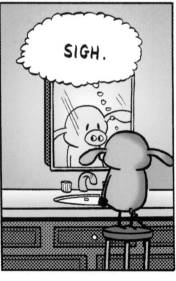

WHAT ARE YOU GUYS DOING?
WE GOT A 'Wii.' WE'VE GOT GOLF, TENNIS, BASE-BALL. NOW WE'RE TRYING OUT THE BOXING.
BAM BAM BAM
YOU DON'T ACTUALLY PUNCH THE OTHER GUY.
OHHHHHHHH.
LET'S TRY GOLF.

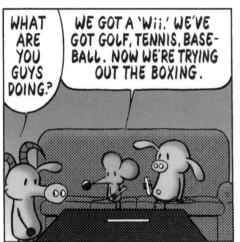

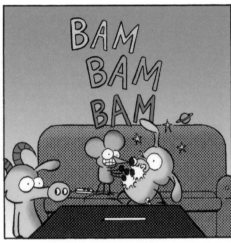

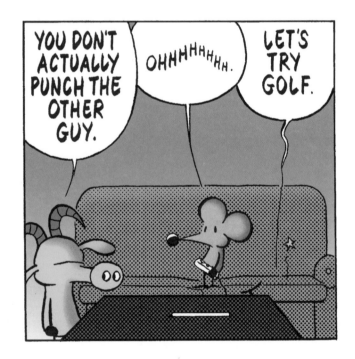

WHAT ARE YOU DOING, LARRY?
Larry hiding. Zeeba neighba have new all-knowing ally called Da Google.
GOOGLE?! GOOGLE'S A SEARCH TOOL.
Dat why me HIDING.
I'M MOVING IN WITH MY MOTHER.
HA! Da Google still find you.

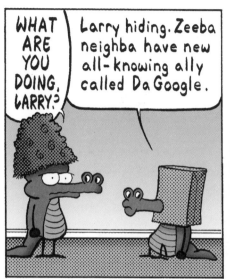

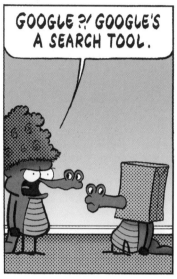

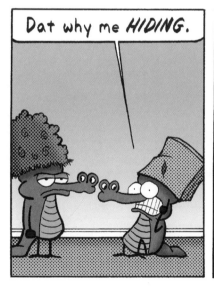

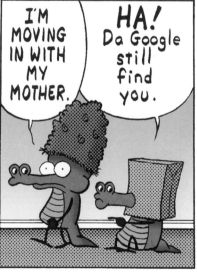

HAVE YOU SEEN YOUR FATHER?
HE'S MEETING WITH THE OTHER CROCS. THEY'RE FORMING A POSSE.
A POSSE? TO DO WHAT?

KEEL DA GOOGLE!
PLEASE CLOSE THE DRAPES.
I'M BETTING ON THE GOOGLE.

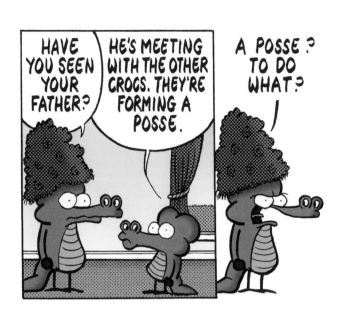

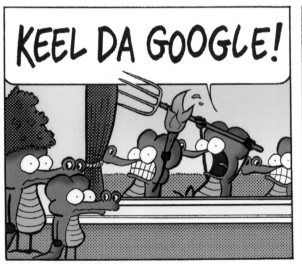

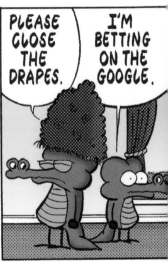

WHAT HAPPENED TO MY LAPTOP?!? IT'S SMASHED TO PIECES!!
It had da Google.
GOOGLE'S ON *EVERY* COMPUTER, DAD.
Whoa... Tell Mom me be late for dinner.

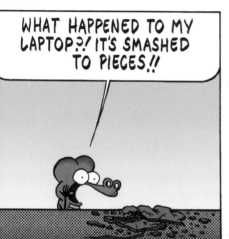

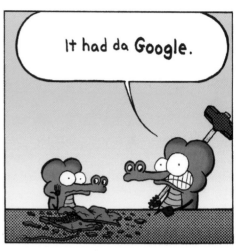

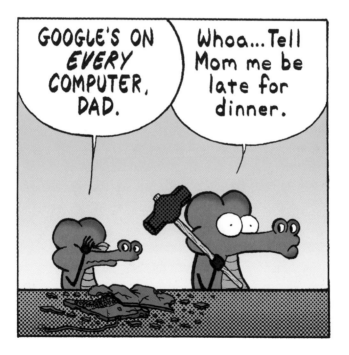

WHAT ARE YOU DOING?
Me showing you Larry top of aneemal food chain, master of all speecies, beeg and small.
Tweet Tweet Tweet
Preetend you no see dat.

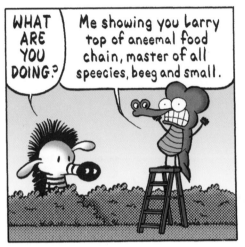

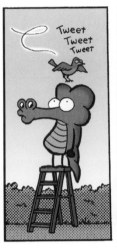

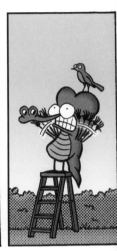

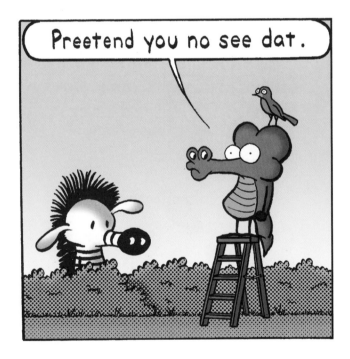

You got bird on hed, Larry.
Me know dat, Bob, so shut mouf. Me no can reech.

Here. Take bat. Hit self een face.
But bird no on face. Bird on hed.

Funnier my way.

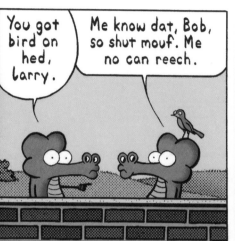

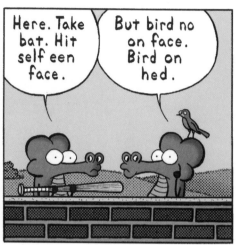

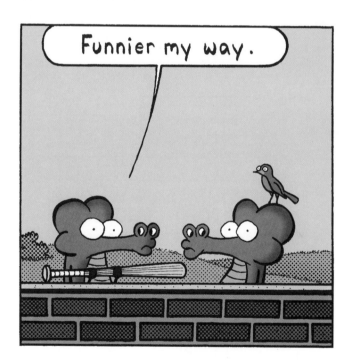

Zeeba!
Save enviromeent
WHAT?
Save enviromeent!
Save enviromeent
WHAT ARE YOU TALKING ABOUT?
Put Bob een you house. Be frend to Bob.
Save enviromeent
WHAT'S THAT HAVE TO DO WITH SAVING THE ENVIRONMENT?
You be Bob frend. Bob green. You green-frendly.
Save enviromeent

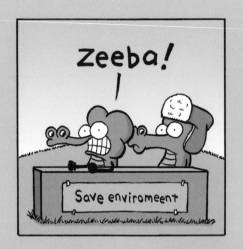

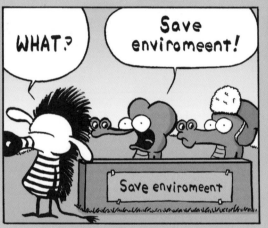

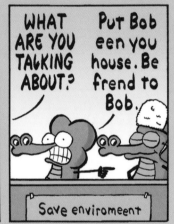

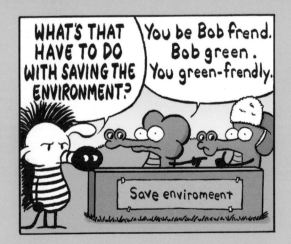

THAT IS *NOT* WHAT GREEN—
Whoa Whoa Whoa. Calm you face down. Have cup o' coffee.
Save enviromeent
IS THAT A POLYSTYRENE FOAM CUP?
Who know? But ees okay 'cause when we done, we trow on ground. Wind blow away.
Save enviromeent
I'M LEAVING NOW.
Hey, Larry, look... Stoopid tree stop cups.
Here. Chop tree down.

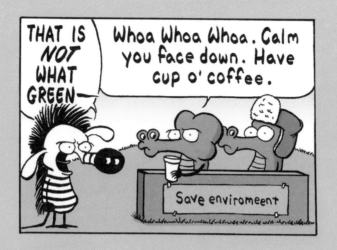

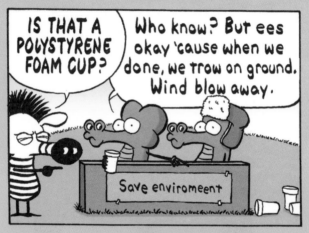

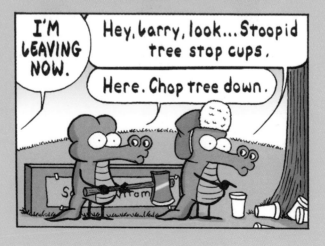

DID YOU KNOW THAT THE MAJORITY OF PEOPLE IN ICELAND BELIEVE IN ELVES?
THAT CAN'T BE TRUE.
IT IS. THEY BELIEVE THAT EACH HOUSE HAS ITS OWN ELF, WHO ONLY GOES OUTSIDE WHEN THE ENERGY IN THE HOUSE BECOMES TOO NEGATIVE.
THAT'S GOTTA BE THE STUPIDEST THING I'VE EVER HEARD.

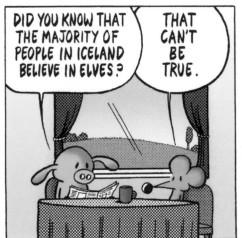

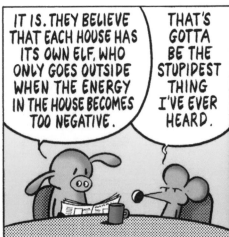

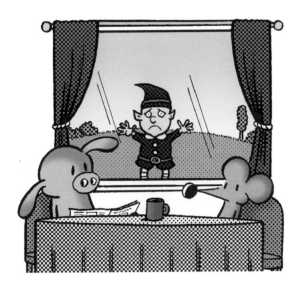

WHY DO YOU HAVE A FAKE OLYMPIC MEDAL AROUND YOUR NECK?
I'M TRAINING. AND THE MEDAL'S FOR INSPIRATION.
Cheese Poofs
POP
'BEING FAT ON THE COUCH' IS NOT AN OLYMPIC EVENT.
Cheese Poofs
YOU'VE KILLED A DREAM.
Cheese Poofs
POP

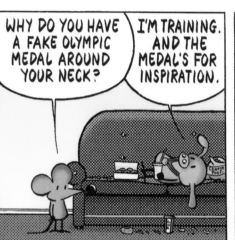

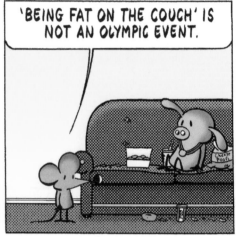

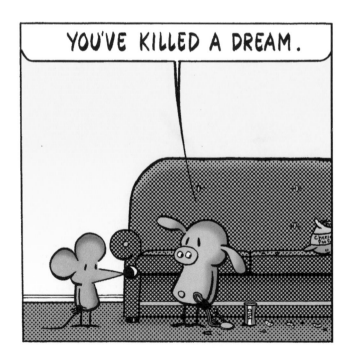

HEY, THERE, ZEBRA... WHY YOU COVERED IN 'SILLY STRING'?
I DON'T THINK THAT'S WHAT SPIDER-MAN USES.
THANKS, PIG. I KNOW.
Hey... Why you no eemobilized?

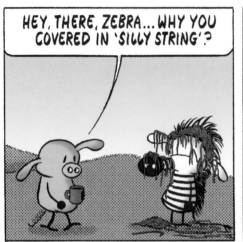

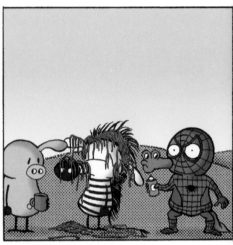

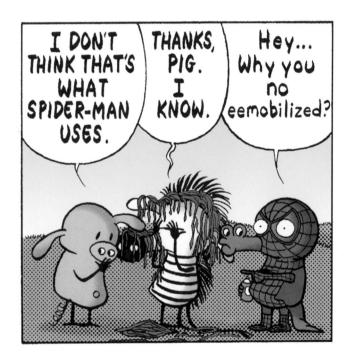

HEY, RAT, LOOK... I WROTE A SHORT STORY.
WOW, PIG... THIS STORY IS POSITIVELY PROSAIC.
REALLY?
CARE TO TELL HIM THAT 'PROSAIC' MEANS DULL?
WHY? THE WORD SOUNDS SO POSITIVE.
"'POSITIVELY PROSAIC,' PROCLAIMS ONE READER."

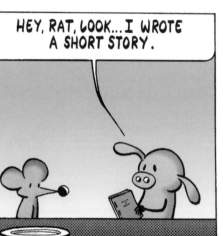

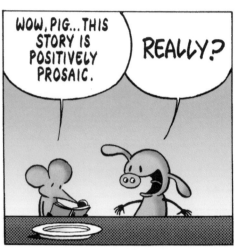

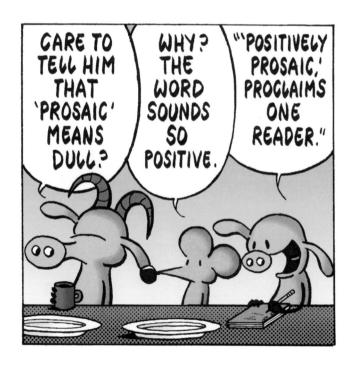

DO YOU THINK FLAMENCO DANCERS ARE INTIMIDATING?
INTIMIDATING?
YEAH... LIKE IF SOMEONE CHALLENGED YOU TO A BAR FIGHT, AND YOU STRUCK A FLAMENCO POSE, WOULD THAT INTIMIDATE THEM?
OF COURSE NOT. IT'S A DANCE.
TOLD YOU.
CARE TO STEP OUTSIDE?
YES. BECAUSE I'M LEAVING.

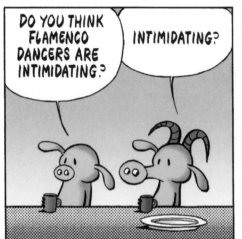

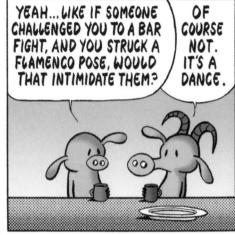

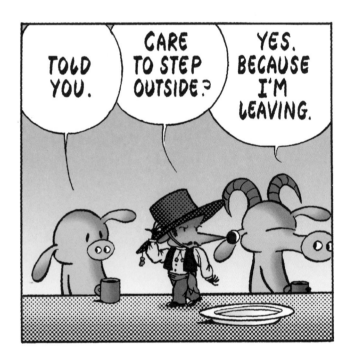

OH, GREAT...WHAT ARE YOU DOING NOW, YOU DUMB PIG? SELLING PEOPLE COMPLIMENTS FOR A BUCK?
NO, I'M BUYING! I GIVE YOU A DOLLAR, SEE, AND YOU SAY SOMETHING NICE ABOUT ME!
Complimints $1.00
A DOLLAR? OH, YOU SAD, LONELY, HOMELY, PATHETIC LARDBUTT.
Complimints $1.00
I'D LIKE A REFUND.
Complimints $1.00

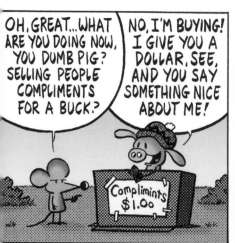

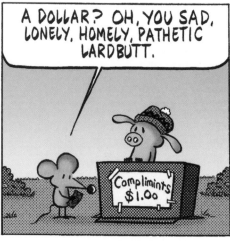

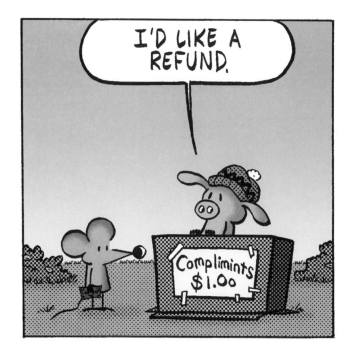

I'M SORRY, RAT, BUT WHY DO YOU ALWAYS PUT THE EMPTY 'POP-TARTS' BOX BACK IN THE CUPBOARD AFTER YOU TAKE THE LAST ONE?
SO THE 'POP-TART' FAIRY WILL REFILL IT.
SO THAT'S HOW THEY GET IN THERE.

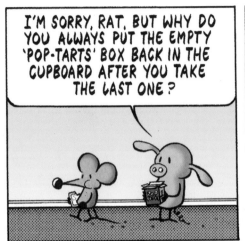

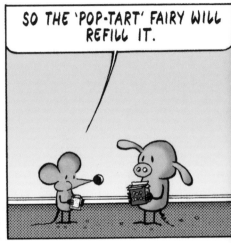

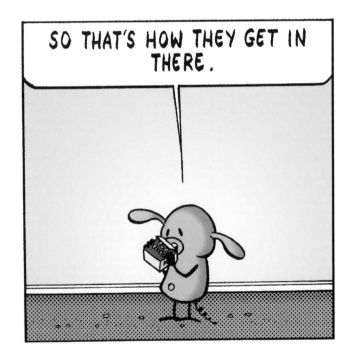

Dear Diary,
    Today I fell into the laundry basket. When I came out, I was Gym Sock Nose Guy. My mission: Harness my superhero powers to defeat the forces of intolerance.

LEAVE, SMELLY.

NO.

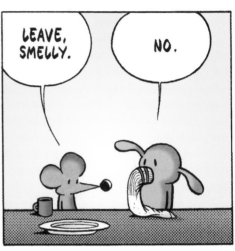

Score one for the good guys.

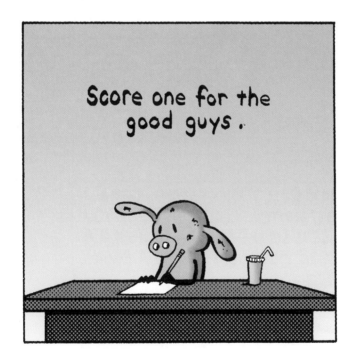

Hulloooo, zeeba neighba. Leesten. We crocs leetle tired you atteetude.
YEAH, WELL, I'VE HAD IT WITH YOU, TOO.
Yeah. Well, we is hate you more. So eeder you is change or Larry here write tell-all book about you and you stoopid face.
YEAH, WELL I SUGGEST YOU GET A GHOST WRITER BECAUSE NONE OF YOU CROCS IS SMART ENOUGH TO *READ* A BOOK, MUCH LESS *WRITE* A BOOK.

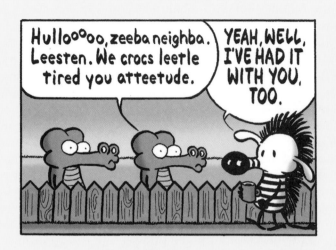

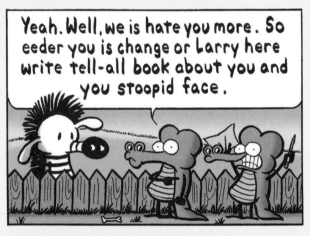

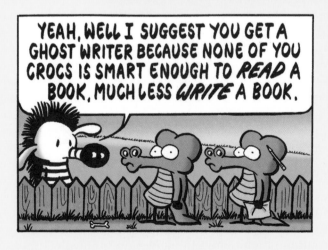

Ohhhhh, we no smart enough, huh? Well, dat EXAKK kind of rudeness we is talk about een book. Right, Larry?
Boo.
Dat no what ghost writer is, Larry.
Gud. 'Cause it hard to write wid sheet on hed, Bob.

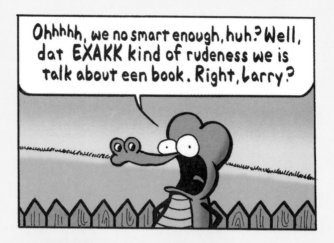

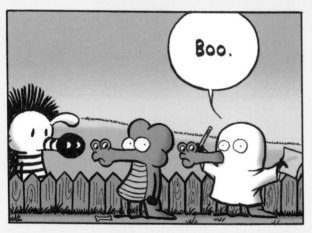

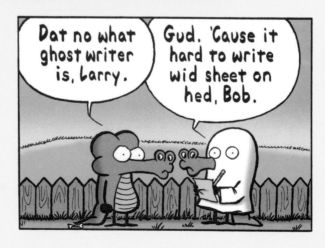

WHAT ARE YOU READING, PIG?
A MAGAZINE ON MODEL TRAINS. I THINK I'M GONNA BUILD MY OWN TRAIN LAYOUT.
MODEL TRAINS
OH, YEAH? I USED TO DO THAT. STANDARD GAUGE OR NARROW? 'O' SCALE? 'G' SCALE? 'S' SCALE?
ONE THAT GOES 'CHOO CHOO.'

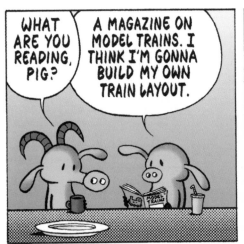

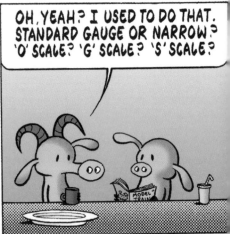

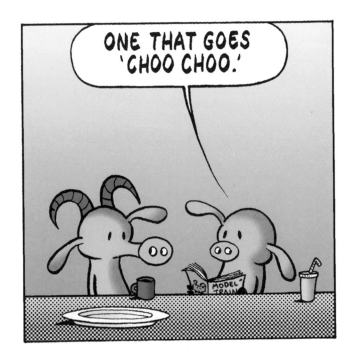

HELLO. I'M J. RUTHERFORD SHRIMP, FOUNDER OF 'SHRIMPS FOR A BETTER FUTURE,' AND I'M CIRCULATING A PETITION TO BAN THE CONSUMPTION OF SHRIMP ON THE GROUND THAT WE ARE LIVING BEINGS WITH RIGHTS THAT MUST BE RESPECTED.
THEN WHY ON EARTH DO THEY EAT YOU?
SIMPLY BECAUSE WE ARE TASTY.
HE HAD ME UP TO TASTY.
CHOMP CHOMP

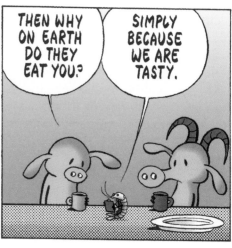

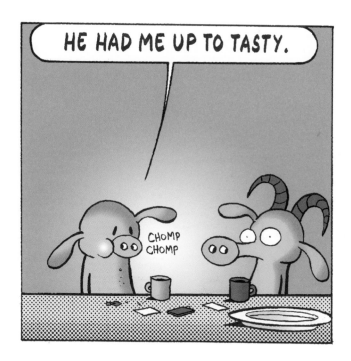

WHAT DO YOU GOT THERE, RAT?
THE TOWEL ROLL O' EVIL, A GIANT PAPER TOWEL ROLL WHERE I KEEP TRACK OF ALL THE BACKSTABBERS AND CONNIVERS WHO HAVE DONE ME WRONG IN LIFE.
BUT NOT EVERYONE IN LIFE IS A BACKSTABBER OR A CONNIVER. SOME PEOPLE ARE LOVING AND HELPFUL. WHERE DO YOU KEEP THEIR NAMES?
THE TOOTSIE ROLL O' KINDNESS.

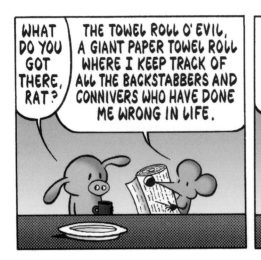

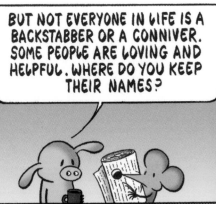

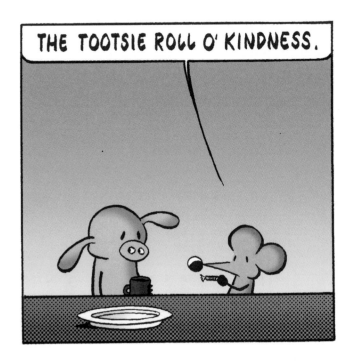

GOSH, I SURE LOVE THIS BOOK...THE AUTHOR'S A REAL MASTER OF DRAMATIC IRONY.
I'M SORRY, PIG... I DON'T MEAN TO SOUND ALL ACADEMIC...DO YOU KNOW WHAT IRONY IS?
OH, YES.
USE IT IN A SENTENCE.
THE CARPENTER'S NAIL FELT VERY IRONY.
OHH BRAVO! BRAVO!
CLAP CLAP
CLAP
CLAP
LANGUAGES IS SORT OF MY STRENGTH.
CHECK PLEASE.

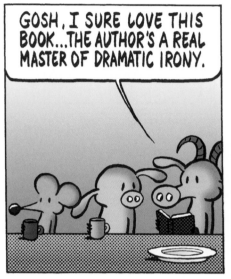

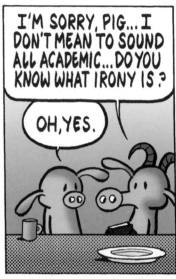

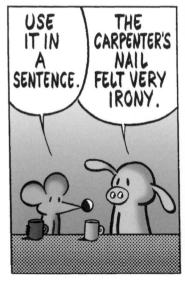

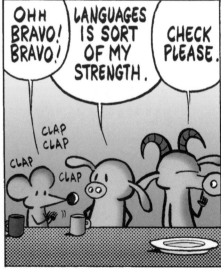

HIYA, RAT...I'D LIKE YOU TO MEET MY NEW FRIEND, JACKO THE FIRE-BREATHING DRAGON.
WHY'S HE SO SMALL?
PITUITARY GLAND PROBLEMS. THEY'VE STIFLED HIS GROWTH.
I'LL SAY. ANYTHING ELSE WRONG WITH HIM?
AAHCHOO
ALLERGIES.

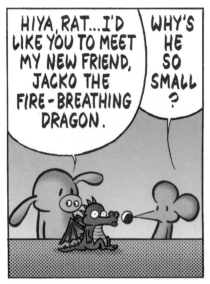

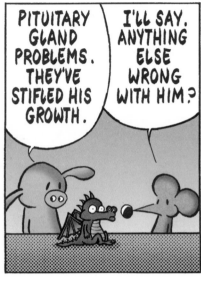

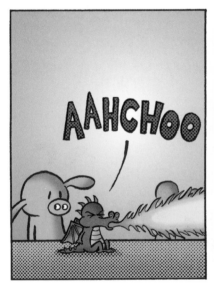

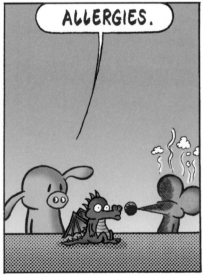

DID YOU KNOW THAT THE MONGOLS ONCE HELD AN EMPIRE THAT STRETCHED FROM THE PACIFIC OCEAN TO THE DANUBE?... HAVE YOU EVER HEARD OF ANYTHING SO AMAZING?
OH, YES.
WHAT?
BRITISH PEOPLE CALL FRENCH FRIES 'CHIPS.'
THIS MIGHT BE WHY WE DON'T DISCUSS HISTORY.
WHAT NEXT— DRIVING ON THE WRONG SIDE OF THE ROAD?!?

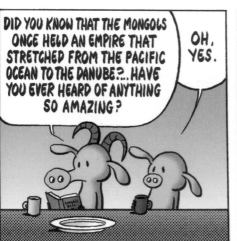

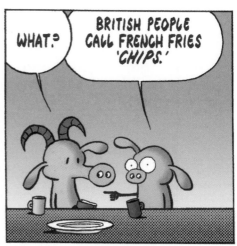

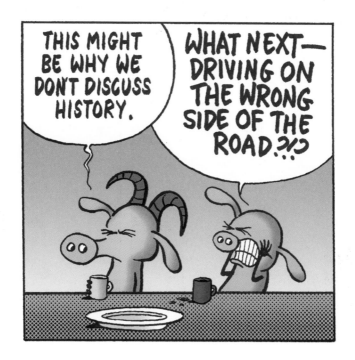

I HAVE FOUNDED AN OPERA COMPANY.
YOU?...WHO DO YOU HAVE THAT CAN SING OPERA?
NOBODY.
THEN WHAT DO YOU HAVE?
A FAT GUY DRESSED FUNNY.
IT'S NINETY PERCENT OF THE BATTLE.

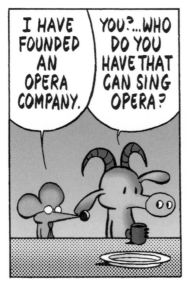

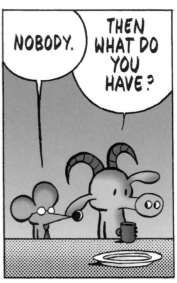

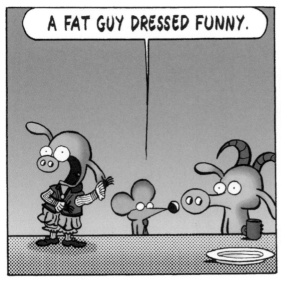

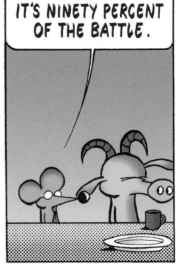

LOOKS LIKE SOMEBODY'S OPENING A FAST FOOD PLACE ON THE CORNER NEAR YOUR HOUSE.
SERVING WHAT ?
SERVING.... ....OH MY.
WHAT IS IT?
Two Zeeba Macs peese.
McZeeba's
You deserve a dead zeeba today

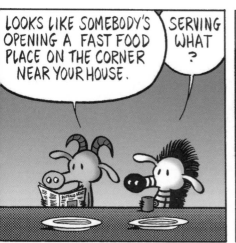

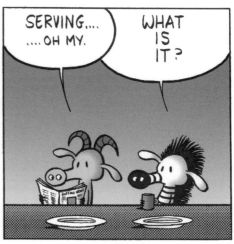

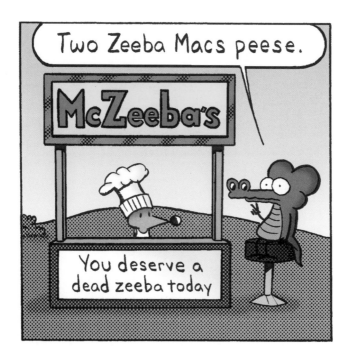

BEHOLD! I, RAT, HAVE FIGURED OUT THAT THE KEY TO HAPPINESS IS TO LOWER YOUR EXPECTATIONS. SO I HAVE CREATED THE 'EXPECTATION CRUSHER.'
HOW'S IT WORK?
EXPECTATION CRUSHER
YOU WRITE DOWN EACH OF YOUR EXPECTATIONS ON THESE STRIPS OF PAPER AND PUT THEM IN HERE. THEN, THE EXPECTATION CRUSHER GRINDS THEM DOWN TO ONE LOW EXPECTATION YOU CAN MEET, MAKING YOU HAPPY! HERE, TRY IT...
EXPECTATION CRUSHER
LET'S SEE...I WANT TO BE LOVED BY EVERYONE..I WANT A MILLION FRIENDS...I WANT MY OWN AMUSEMENT PARK...I WANT A THOUSAND PONIES.
EXPECTATION CRUSHER

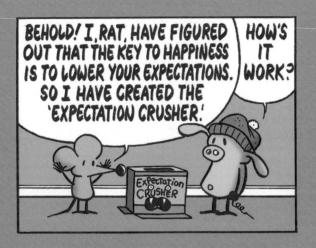

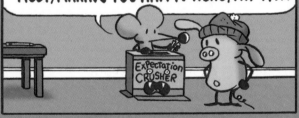

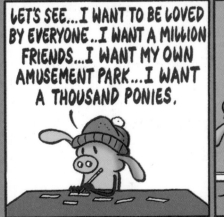

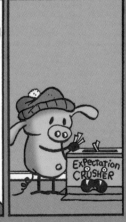

CLICK
CRUSH
CRUSH
CRUSH
GRIND
GRIND
GRIND
Expectation CRUSHER
SPEW
'I WANT A HAT.'
I'VE GOT THAT! I'VE GOT THAT!
HOW DID YOU DO THAT?

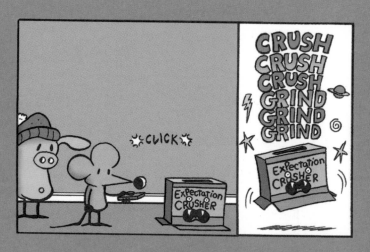

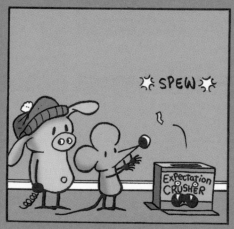

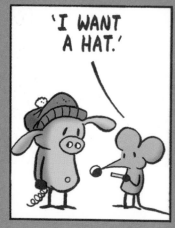

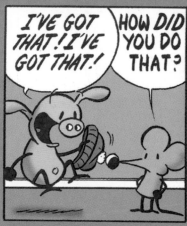

WHAT ARE YOU DOING, RAT?
BRINGING ZEBRA MEAT TO THE MASSES.
McZeeba's
You deserve a dead zeeba today
BUT YOU'RE FRIENDS WITH A ZEBRA.
YOU EAT BACON.
BACON TASTES GOOD.
ZEEBA MACS TASTE GREAT.
OKAY... JUST ONE MORE BITE.

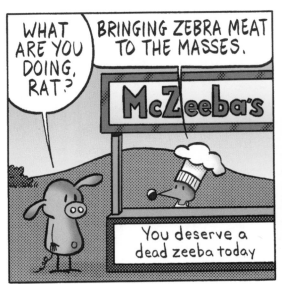

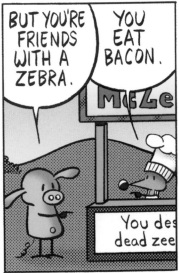

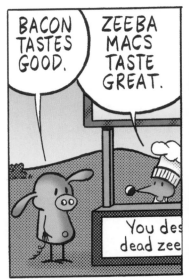

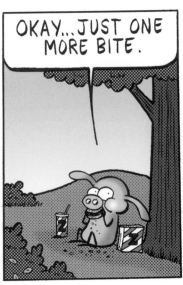

WHAT HAPPENED HERE?
My frend Bob choke on you Zeeburger... It have beeg bone.
McZeebas
OH MY.
Yeah... You keel my bess frend... Whuh you do now?
McZeebas
COMPLIMENTARY NACHOS?
Ooooooooh... Extra cheesy.
McZeebas

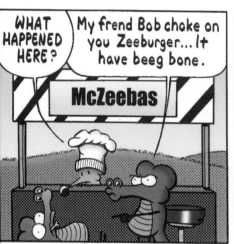

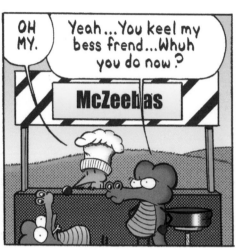

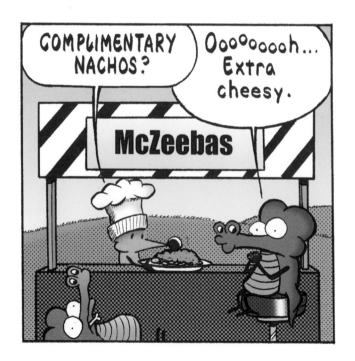

WHAT ARE YOU DOING, PIG?
I'M WEARING MAGIC PANTS.
THEY'RE YOUR MONKEY PAJAMA BOTTOMS. AND YOU'VE PULLED THEM UP TO YOUR NECK.
NO. THEY'RE MAGIC PANTS. AND THE HIGHER I WEAR THEM, THE MAGIC-ER I AM.
THAT'S TOO HIGH.

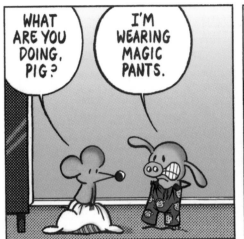

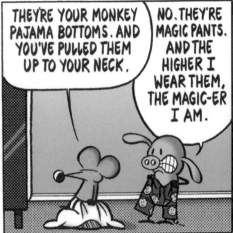

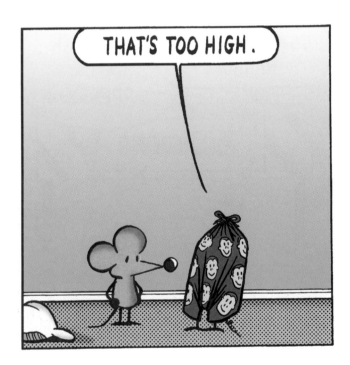

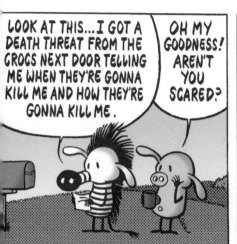

LOOK AT THIS... I GOT A DEATH THREAT FROM THE CROCS NEXT DOOR TELLING ME WHEN THEY'RE GONNA KILL ME AND HOW THEY'RE GONNA KILL ME.

OH MY GOODNESS! AREN'T YOU SCARED?

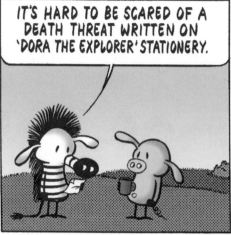

IT'S HARD TO BE SCARED OF A DEATH THREAT WRITTEN ON 'DORA THE EXPLORER' STATIONERY.

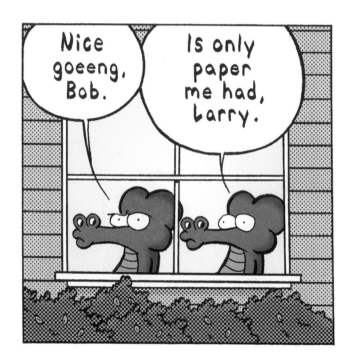

Nice goeeng, Bob.

Is only paper me had, Larry.

THE CROCS REMODELED THEIR HOUSE.
OH, YEAH? WHAT, TO MAKE IT BIGGER? MORE MODERN?
I'D STAY OUT OF THERE.
Which one you Gretel?

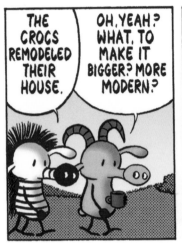

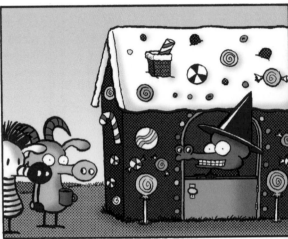

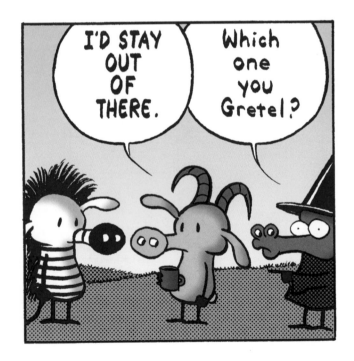

WHAT ARE YOU WRITING, GOAT?
A LETTER TO MY PEN PAL. HE LIVES IN WALES.
THE COUNTRY, NOT THE SEA CREATURES.
OHHHHHHHH.

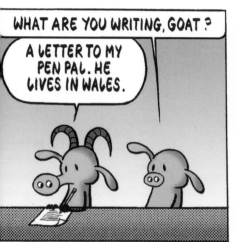

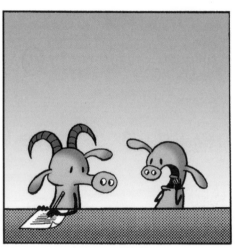

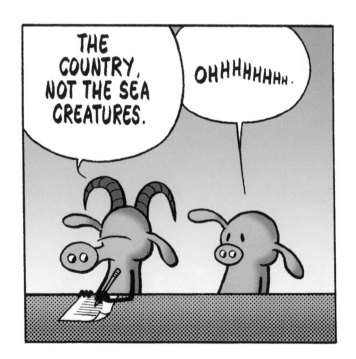

HI, GOAT. I WANT TO GIVE YOU SOMETHING.
DO YOU MIND? I'M TRYING TO FINISH A LETTER.
I KNOW. THAT'S WHY I WANT TO GIVE YOU THIS. IT'S A PLAQUE CERTIFYING YOU AS THE LAST LETTER-WRITER IN AMERICA. CONGRATULATIONS.
GO AWAY.
OH, AND THE PRIZE INCLUDES THIS FINE OIL LAMP AND A BUGGY WHIP.

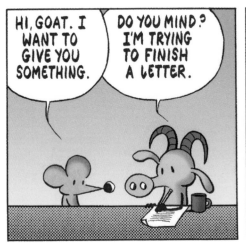

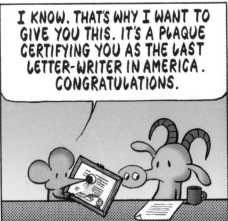

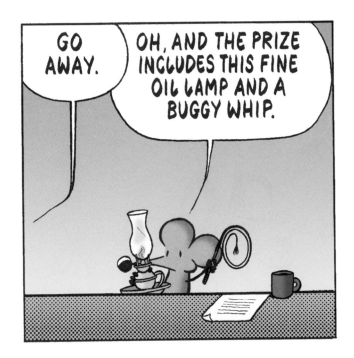

EXCUSE ME, SIR...CAN I GIVE YOU THIS?
WHAT IS IT?
WHAT DO YOU MEAN, 'WHAT IS IT?'...IT'S A LETTER TO A FRIEND.
OH, YEAAAAH... I REMEMBER THESE.
I GIVE UP.
OH, WELL...I'M OFF TO DELIVER SOME MORE 'NETFLIX' ENVELOPES.

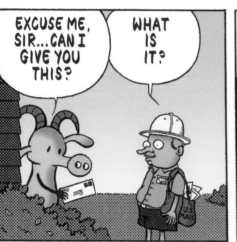

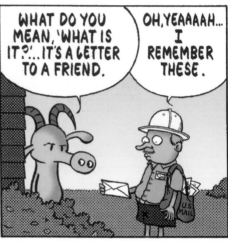

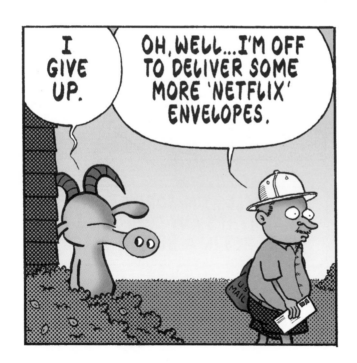

Hullo, zeeba neighba.
WHY ARE YOU ALL DRESSED UP?
Meemorial service for cousin Nick. He die.
OH... WELL... I'M SORRY TO HEAR THAT. IF IT'S ANY COMFORT, I'M SURE HE'S IN A BETTER PLACE.

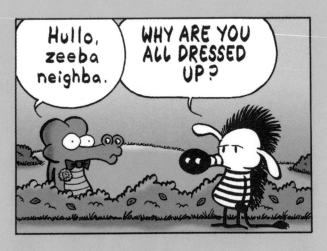

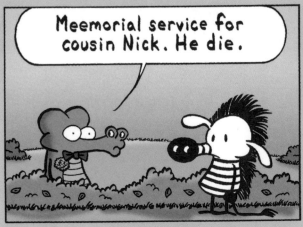

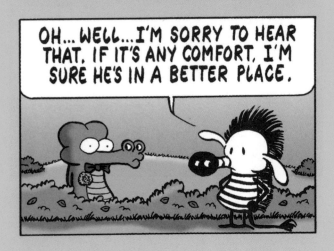

Yeah. Me sure too.
ON YOUR FEET.
HOW YOU LIKE AFTERLIFE, NICK?

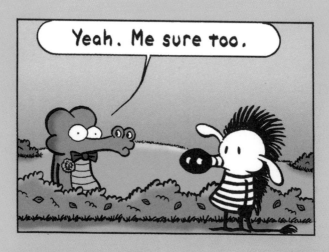

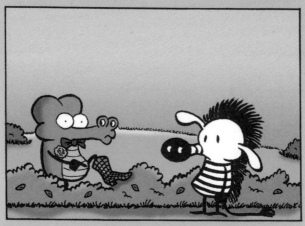

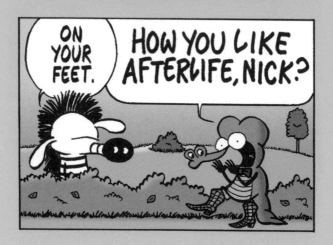

WHAT DO YOU GOT THERE, PIG?
IT'S MY DECEASED FRIEND, WILLY THE WOODPECKER. I GUESS HE JUST WORE HIMSELF OUT CONSTANTLY BANGING HIS FOREHEAD INTO A TREE.
WOODPECKERS DON'T USE THEIR FOREHEADS. THEY USE THEIR BEAKS.
WILLY WOULD HAVE FOUND THAT INFORMATION USEFUL.

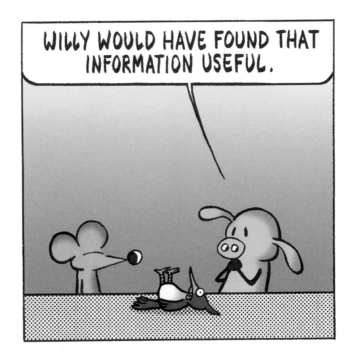

Well, woomun, look like zeeba try deeg seecret tunnel out of hees house, but ees okay, becuss me has Bob cover exit hole.
THAT'S A FIRE ANT MOUND.
Dat bad news for Bob.

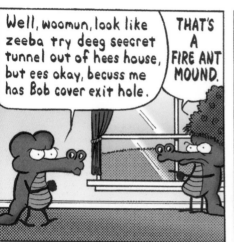

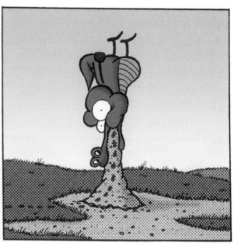

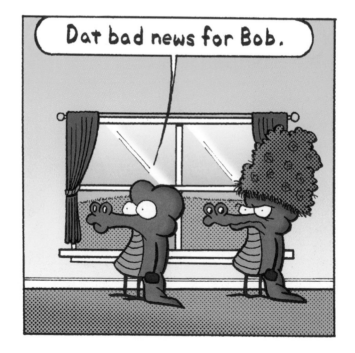

GOOD AFTERNOON, ZEBRA. AS YOU MAY NOTICE, I'VE HAD MY SPEECH NOTABLY IMPROVED BY GENETIC ENGINEERING, A RISKY PROCEDURE THAT EITHER GREATLY ENHANCES OR DIMINISHES THE GENES THAT CONTROL SPEECH. BOB HERE HAS HAD THE PROCEDURE ALSO.
Wubba. Wubba. Koosh. Koosh.
HIS WAS NOT AS SUCCESSFUL.

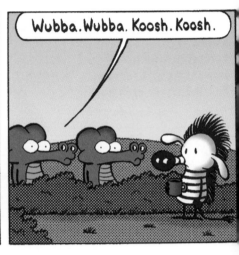

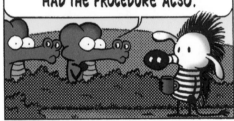

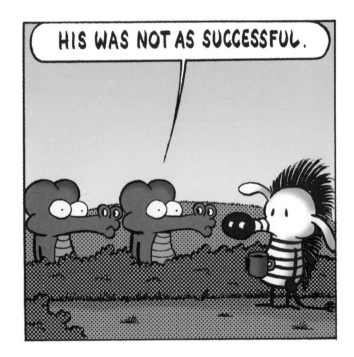

PIG, I'VE DECIDED THAT WITH YOUR DIM PROSPECTS, YOU SHOULD LIVE LIFE BACKWARDS. TURN YOUR BACK UPON THE PAINFUL PRESENT AND UNSIGHTLY FUTURE AND GAZE SOLELY UPON THE JOY THAT WAS THE PAST.

I DIDN'T HAVE A JOYFUL PAST.

I'VE DECIDED YOU SHOULD LIVE LIFE IN A BURLAP BAG.

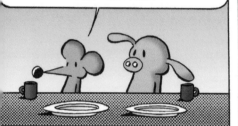

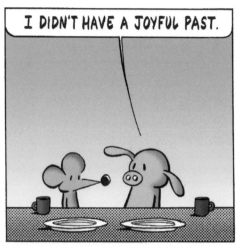

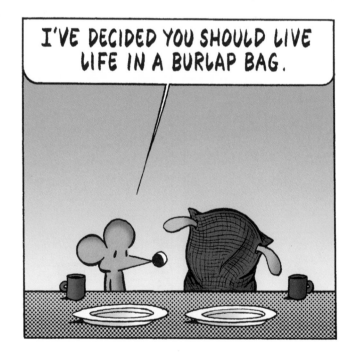

HEY, ZEBRA, WHAT CAN I DO FOR YOU?
HI, PIG...I'M CIRCULATING A PETITION TO BAN REPTILES FROM THE NEIGHBORHOOD. CARE TO SIGN?
ABSOLUTELY NOT. WE'VE GOT SOME IN OUR BATHROOM.
SINCE WHEN DO YOU HAVE THEM IN YOUR BATHROOM?
SINCE WE RE-DID THE COUNTER.
REPTILES. NOT RED TILES.
RIPPED TILES? I SHOULD HOPE NOT. THEY'RE NEW.

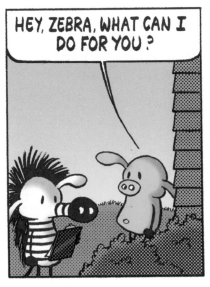

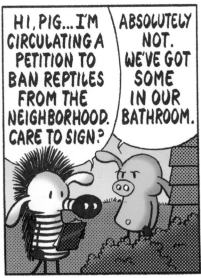

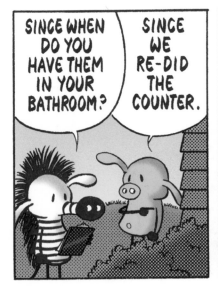

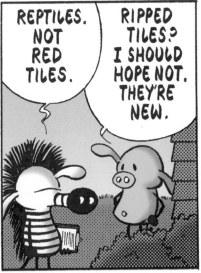

WHAT ARE YOU DOING OVER THERE?
We play game of peeckle wid Bob.
OH, YEAH? WHERE YOU THROW THE BALL BETWEEN TWO BASES AND HAVE TO TAG THE RUNNERS?

No.

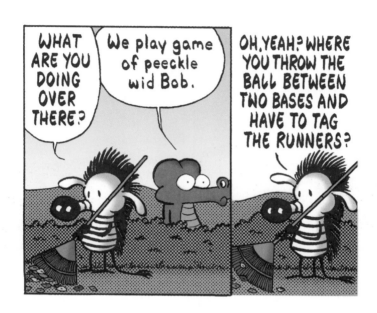

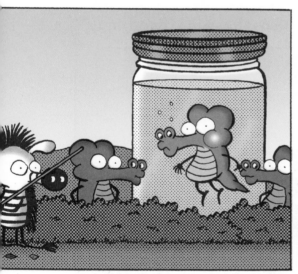

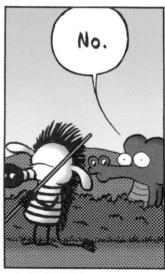

WHAT ARE YOU GUYS DOING?
Ees 'Croc Een A Box'! Ees latest trend! Buy! Put een house!
Croc Een A Box
WHY WOULD I PUT A CROCODILE IN MY HOUSE?!
Ooooh...You drive hard bargain...Okay...Buy now and me trow een second 'Croc Een Box' free.
Croc Een A Box
Croc Een A Box
GO AWAY.
Wow. You reely pushing luck. But okay, me trow een sheeping handling.
Croc Een A Box

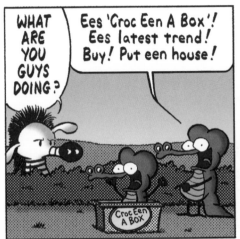

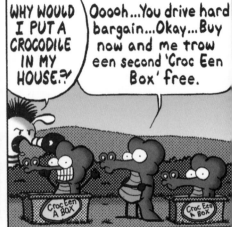

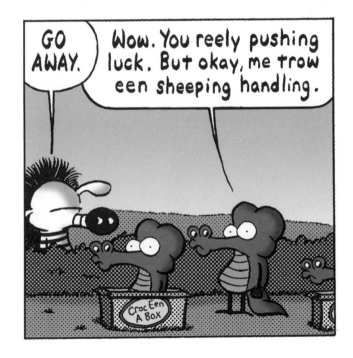

WHY ARE WE OUT HERE?
BECAUSE I HAVE BEEN WATCHING 'MAN VS. WILD' AND I HAVE LEARNED ALL THE TECHNIQUES FOR SURVIVING IN NATURE'S HARSHEST CLIMATES WITH NOTHING BUT YOUR SKILL TO SEPARATE YOU FROM AN OTHERWISE CERTAIN DEATH.
MAY I GO INSIDE FOR A SODA POP?
YOU'RE REALLY RUINING THE EXPERIENCE.

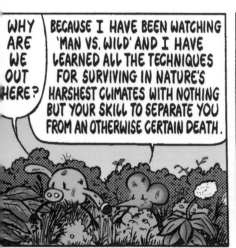

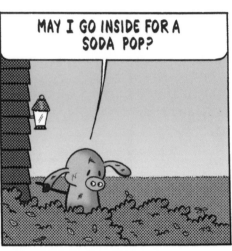

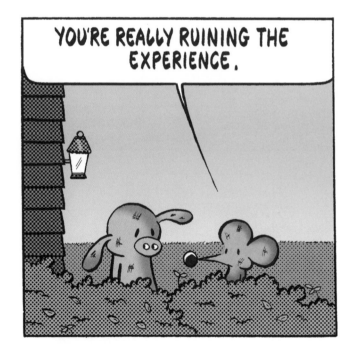

IF SOMEONE PUTS SOMETHING IN A BOOK AND TELLS YOU IT'S TRUE, THEN IT'S GUARANTEED TO BE TRUE, RIGHT?
NO, PIG. PEOPLE CAN LIE IN BOOKS JUST AS THEY CAN ANYWHERE ELSE.
BUT IF A MAGAZINE SAYS IT, IT'S TRUE, RIGHT?
NO, NOT NECESSARILY.
A NEWSPAPER?
NO, NOT NECESSARILY.

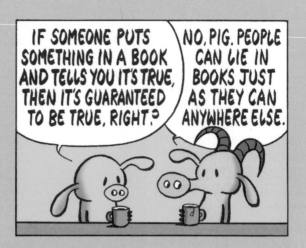

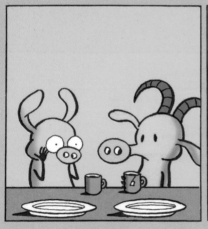

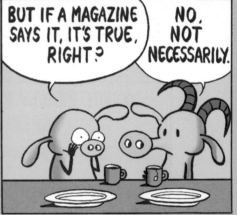

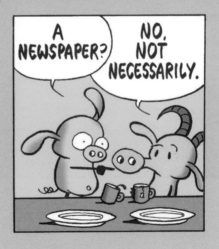

MY MOM?!
GEE, PIG, YOU KNOW, EVEN MOMS SOMETIMES HAVE TO...
AAAHHHHHHHH!! MY VERY BEST FRIEND IN THE WHOLE UNIVERSE, MR. PITTERS?!!
CAN MR. PITTERS TALK?
NO.
THEN YES. MR. PITTERS NEVER LIES TO YOU.
I KNEW WE WERE BEST FRIENDS FOR A REASON.

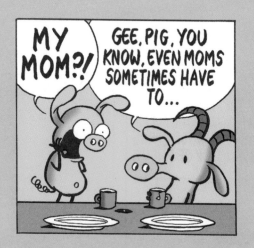

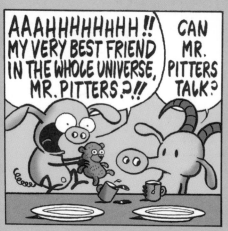

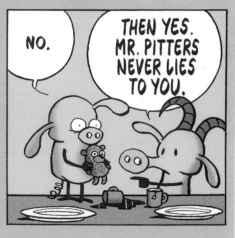

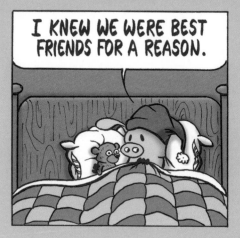

HEY, RAT... I'D LIKE YOU TO MEET MY FRIEND, FOOFY THE FLYING FISH.
FLYING FISH CAN'T REALLY FLY. THEY'RE JUST CALLED THAT BECAUSE THEY LEAP OUT OF THE WATER, GIVING THE *ILLUSION* OF FLIGHT.

PLOP

FOOFY DIDN'T NEED TO KNOW THAT.

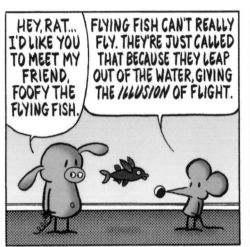

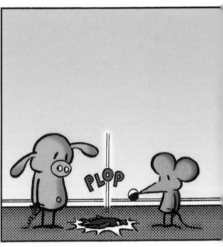

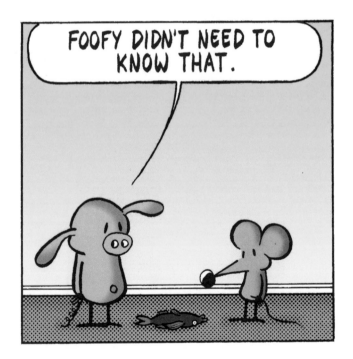

WHAT ARE YOU DOING, RAT?
PLAYING TIMMY THE HOUSEFLY IN DARTS. I DON'T KNOW WHAT THE GUY'S PROBLEM IS, BUT THE IDIOT KEEPS MISSING THE BOARD.
I'M TELLING YOU, THIS IS VERY HARD WITH COMPOUND EYES.
THROW THE DART, EXCUSÉ BOY.

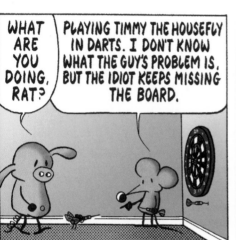

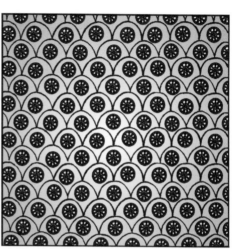

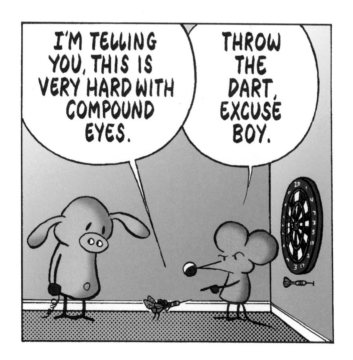

HEY, RAT... WANT TO HELP ME DO MY NEW JIGSAW PUZZLE?...I'VE BEEN AT IT ALL DAY.
PUZZLE
DUDE, I'VE GOT BETTER THINGS TO DO THAN WASTE MY TIME ON SOME 1,000 PIECE MONSTROSITY.
OH, I DON'T LIKE THOSE EITHER, SO I BUY THE ONES THAT ARE A LITTLE EASIER.
PUZZLE
I'M OPEN TO SUGGESTIONS.
PUZZLE

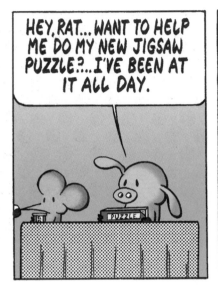

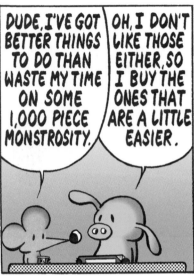

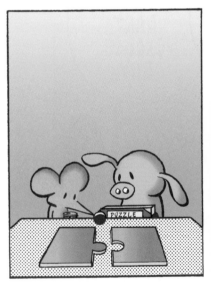

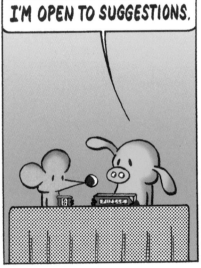

WHAT DO YOU WANT PEOPLE TO SAY ABOUT YOU AFTER YOU'RE GONE?
DEPENDS. WHERE'D I GO?
YOU'RE IN THE GROUND.
AM I DIGGING FOR SOMETHING?
YOU'RE DEAD.
NUTS. MUST HAVE STRAINED MYSELF DIGGING.

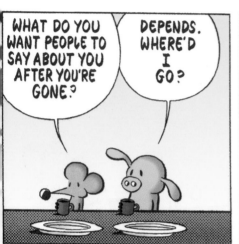

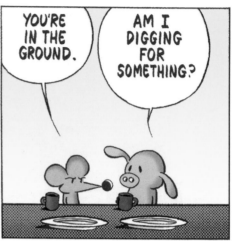

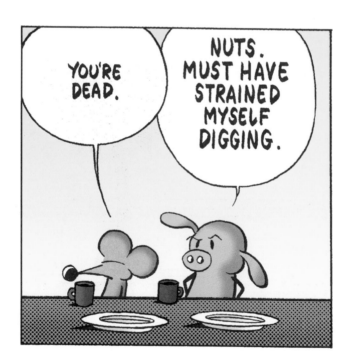

WHAT ARE YOU READING, GOAT?
THIS MAGAZINE ON KITCHEN REMODELS. I'M THINKING ABOUT HAVING A CONTRACTOR INSTALL ONE OF THOSE ISLANDS IN THE CENTER.
WHAT FOR?
IT HELPS WITH THE RESALE VALUE OF THE HOME. THEY'RE A VERY POPULAR FEATURE RIGHT NOW.
HELPS WITH RESALE.

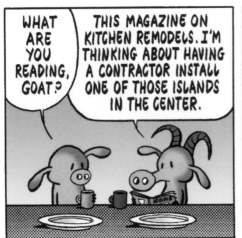

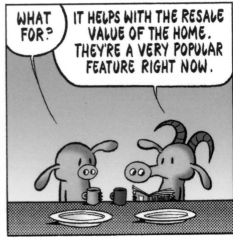

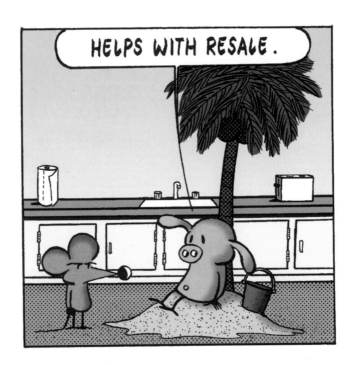

ONE, TWO, THREE, FOUR...NUTS...I LANDED ON B+O RAILROAD.
WHY IS THAT BAD? I DON'T OWN IT.
BECAUSE IT MEANS I SMELL AND HAVE TO GET PUNCHED IN THE NOSE.
NO, IT DOESN'T, PIG. WHERE'D YOU HEAR THAT?!
MONOPOLY
I THINK IT'S IN THE RULES.
IT IS NOT IN THE RULES.
HEY, IT BEATS WHAT HAPPENS WHEN I GO DIRECTLY TO JAIL.

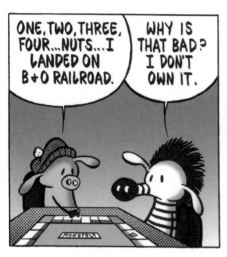

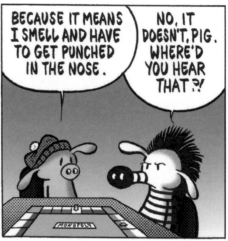

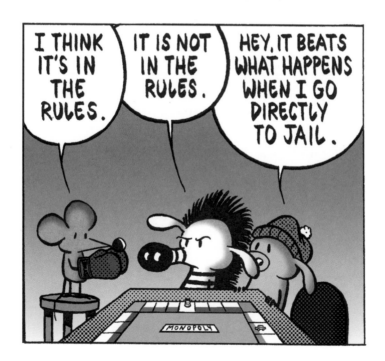

WELL, I THINK I FINALLY FINISHED PAINTING THE LIVING ROOM.
DID YOU KNOW THE WORD 'PAINT' COMES FROM THE OLD FRENCH WORD, 'PEINTIER,' WHICH COMES FROM THE LATIN, 'PINGERE'?
WHAT ARE YOU DOING?
CONFIRMING GOAT'S STORIES REALLY ARE AS BORING AS WATCHING PAINT DRY.

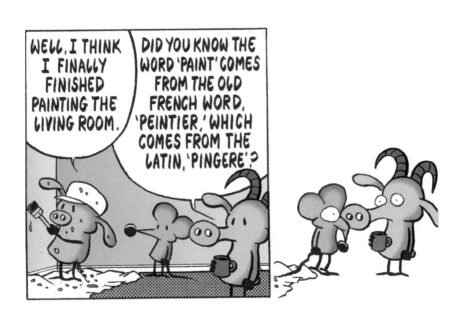

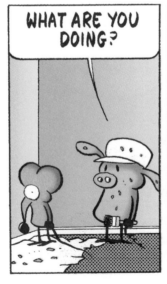

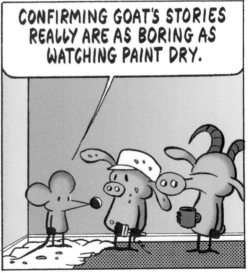

DID GEORGE WASHINGTON HAVE A POINT AT THE TOP OF HIS HEAD?
NO.
WAS HE FIVE HUNDRED FEET TALL?
NO.
FAMOUS MONUMENTS
THE WASHINGTON MONUMENT DOES NOT DEPICT GEORGE WASHINGTON.
THEN WHO'S THAT S'POSED TO BE?
IT'S HIS ARCH NEMESIS, ANDY OBELISK!

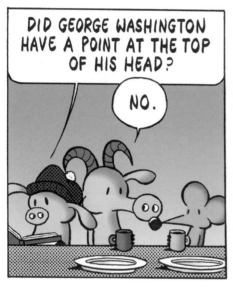

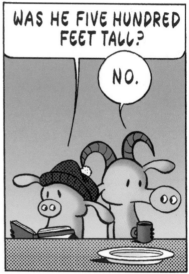

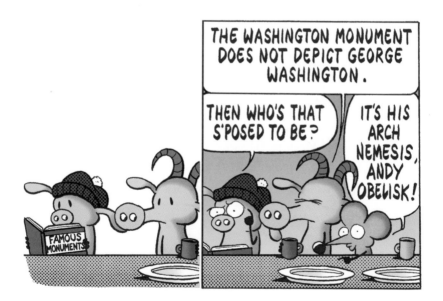

KSSHHHH
THUD
WHAT THE HECK WAS THAT?
A BRICK. LOOKS LIKE SOMEONE WAS TRYING TO KILL US.

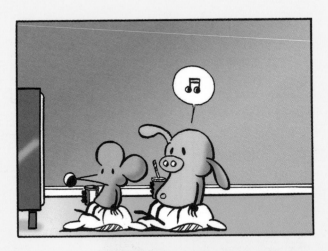

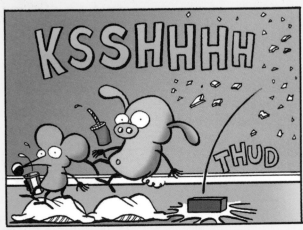

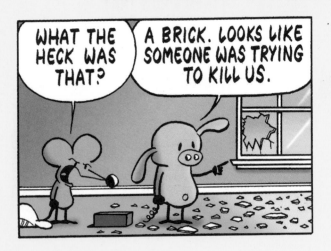

LOOK, THERE'S A NOTE...READ IT.

'PLEASE RETURN YOUR OVERDUE BOOKS.'

WE HAVE SERIOUS LIBRARIANS.

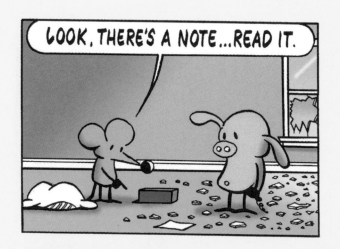

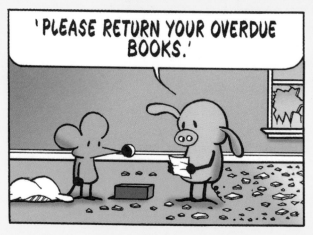

DO YOU THINK THAT HAVING CHORES YOU HAVE TO DO EVERY WEEK MAKES YOU A MORE RESPONSIBLE GUY?
OH, YES. AND THE MORE RESPONSIBLE YOU ARE, THE BETTER ALL-AROUND BEING YOU ARE, WHICH IN TURN MAKES YOU HAPPY.
YEAH. AND I *WANT* TO BE HAPPY AND ALL, BUT...WELL...
...IT'S MORE IMPORTANT TO ME THAT...
POP
POP
...YOU BE HAPPY.
SIGH

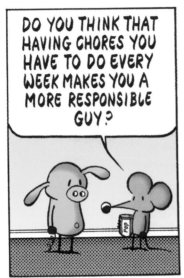

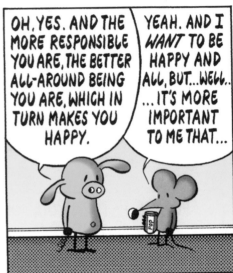

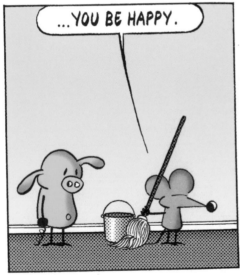

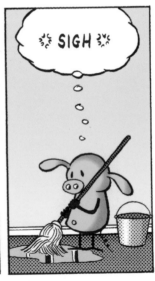

WHAT DO YOU GOT THERE, RAT?
PACKAGE FROM AUSTRALIA. I'M TIRED OF MY RELIANCE ON OIL AND WANTED TO EXPLORE SOME ENERGY ALTERNATIVES.
WELL, GOOD FOR YOU, RAT...YEAH, I THINK AUSTRALIA'S A REAL PIONEER IN PRACTICAL ENERGY OPTIONS WE CAN ALL UTILIZE, LIKE SOLAR AND WIND AND —
YOU'RE BORING MY KANGAROO.

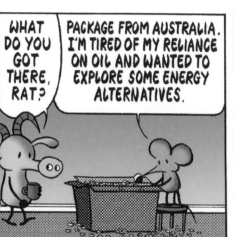

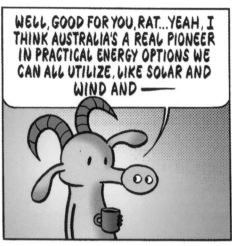

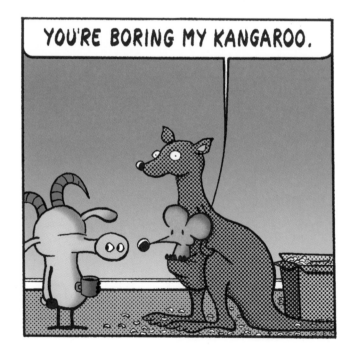

WHAT'S THE MATTER WITH YOU, PIG?
THEY AWARDED THE NOBEL PRIZE IN PHYSICS TO THESE GUYS WHO 'DISCOVERED THE MECHANISM OF BROKEN SYMMETRY IN SUBATOMIC PHYSICS.'
THE DAILY PRESS
WHAT'S WRONG WITH THAT?
THEY STIFFED THE TOASTER INVENTOR AGAIN!!
THIS MIGHT BE WHY WE DON'T DISCUSS PHYSICS.
BREAD GOES IN. TOAST COMES OUT. BEAT THAT!

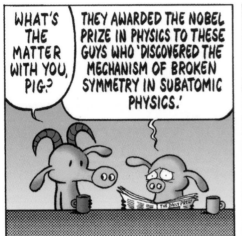

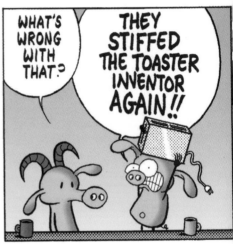

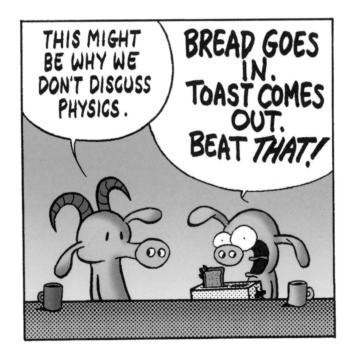

THERE'S A BOY AT THE DOOR WHO WANTS TO SELL US COOKIES TO RAISE MONEY FOR A WORTHY CAUSE.
WHAT'S THE CAUSE?
SURGICAL REMOVAL OF UNWANTED HAIR. HE SAYS IT'S A PROBLEM FOR MILLIONS.
OH, PLEASE. SINCE WHEN IS THE REMOVAL OF AN UNWANTED MUSTACHE OR UNIBROW A WORTHY CAUSE?
WE'LL PASS.
COOKIE

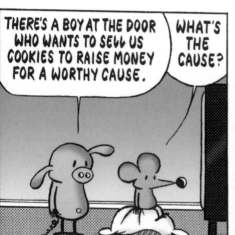

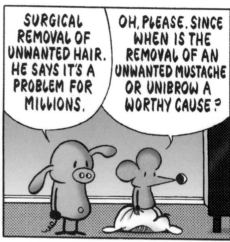

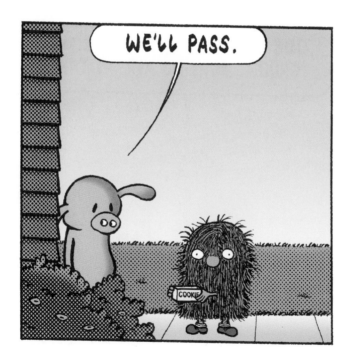

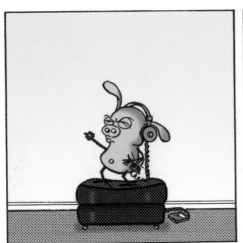
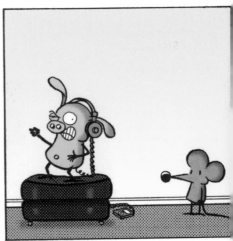

ONE NEVER GETS OVER BEING CAUGHT PLAYING AIR GUITAR.

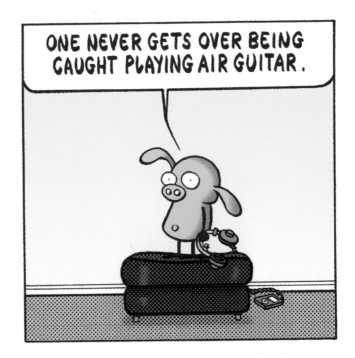

Okay, zeeba neighba, crocs sick of no catching you. So we ees spend money, get some wheels.
OH, YEAH? SO YOU GUYS FINALLY GOT A CAR?
No. Juss some wheels.
He walking away, Bob.
Quick, throw you wheel.

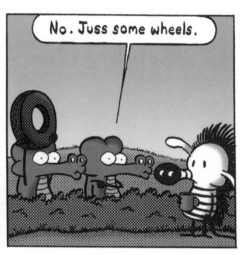

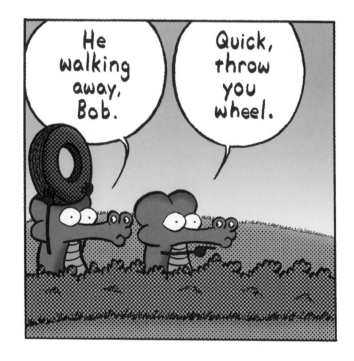

YOU AND I SHOULD BRAINSTORM ABOUT HOW WE CAN MAKE MORE MONEY.
I'D LIKE TO, BUT I CAN'T BRAINSTORM.
WHAT DO YOU MEAN YOU CAN'T BRAIN-STORM?
I CAN ONLY BRAIN CHANCE OF SCATTERED SHOWERS.
NEVER MIND.
AND THE TEN-DAY FORECAST IS NOT GOOD.

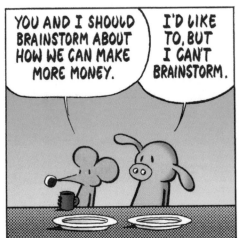

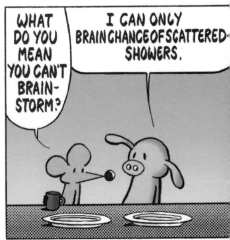

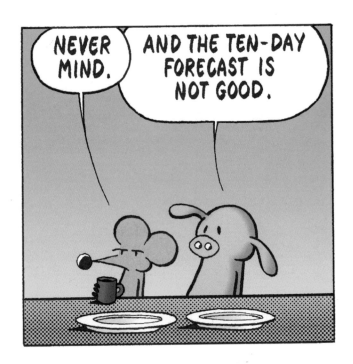

WHAT ARE YOU DOING?
EDITING THE DICTIONARY. I'M CROSSING OUT WORDS WE DON'T NEED ANYMORE AND REPLACING THEM WITH ONES WE DO. THE FIRST TO GET THE AXE WAS 'FORTNIGHT.'
WHAT'S WRONG WITH 'FORTNIGHT'?
UNNECESSARY. NORMAL PEOPLE SAY 'TWO WEEKS.' IT'S ONLY PUR-POSE IS TO MAKE POMPOUS PEOPLE FEEL POMPOUSER.
SINCE WHEN IS 'POMPOUSER' A WORD?
SINCE IT REPLACED 'FORTNIGHT.'
YOU ARE NOT REPLACING 'FORTNIGHT.'
WHOA. YOU'RE SOUNDING POMPOUSER AND POMPOUSER.

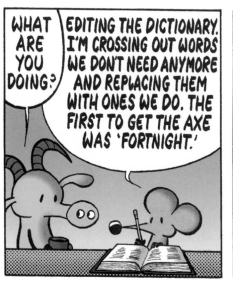

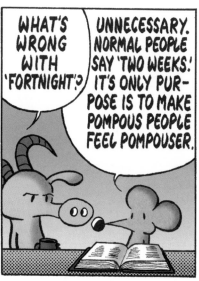

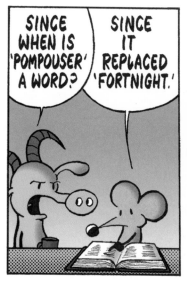

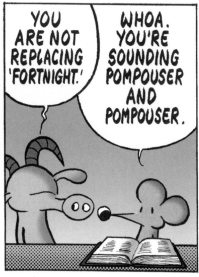

HEY, PIG...WHY YOU SO LATE THIS MORNING?
BLAH BLAH BLAH BLAH BLAH
BLAH BLAH BLAH BLAH BLAH
I WAS AT THE PLASTIC SURGEON'S OFFICE...I'M THINKING ABOUT GET-TING SOME WORK DONE.
WORK, HUH? WHAT KIND OF WORK?
JUST ON MY FACE...EYES, NOSE, YOU KNOW? BUT THE DOCTOR LIKES YOU TO GO THROUGH THIS INITIAL CONSULTATION FIRST.
MUST HAVE BEEN A LONG CONSULT-ATION.

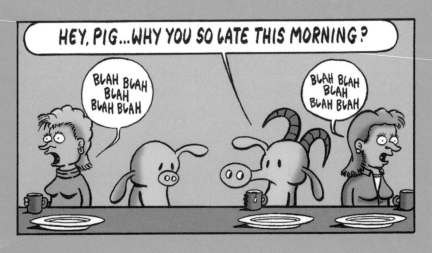

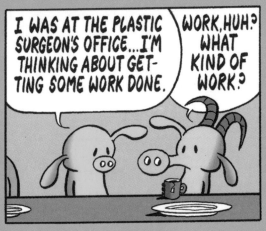

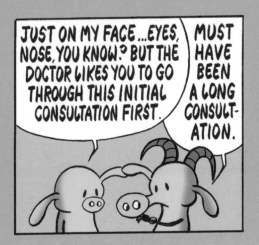

YEAH, HE'S GOT THIS BIG CATALOG OF DIFFERENT FACIAL FEATURES TO CHOOSE FROM. I SPENT THE FIRST HALF HOUR JUST TRYING TO PICK MY NEW EYES.
OH, YEAH? WHAT ELSE DID YOU DO?... AND SPEAK UP A LITTLE... IT'S SO CROWDED IN HERE TODAY.
I SPENT TWO HOURS PICKING MY NOSE!!
HEY, IT LOOKS LIKE THE CROWD'S CLEARING OUT.
I DON'T KNOW HIM.

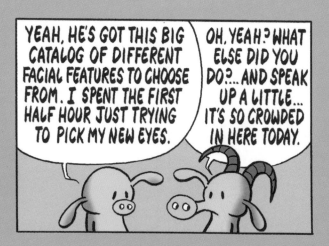

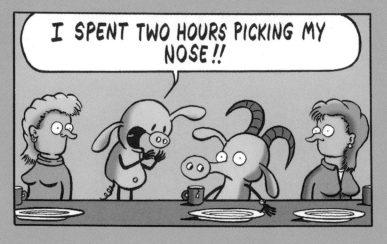

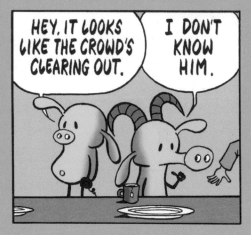

Hullooo, zeeba neighba... Whuh you doeeng?
LISTEN, I DON'T MEAN TO BE OFFENSIVE, BUT WHERE DID YOU GUYS LEARN TO SPEAK ENGLISH?
Same place million guys learn... 'Sesame Street.'
THAT'S RIDICULOUS. I WATCHED 'SESAME STREET' AND I SPEAK FINE. WHAT PART WERE YOU WATCHING?
ME WANT COOKIE!
ME WANT COOKIE TOO!

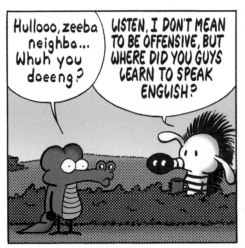

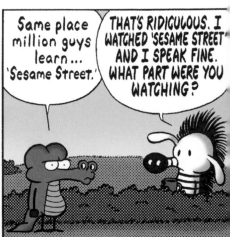

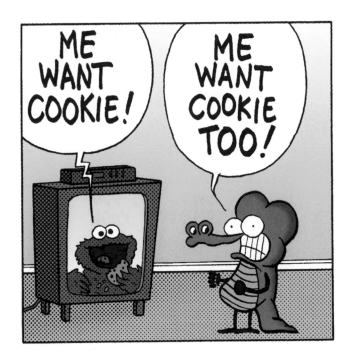

WHAT ARE YOU DOING, RAT?
WRITING IN MY DIARY. I LIKE TO KEEP TRACK OF HOW AWESOME I WAS EACH DAY ON A SCALE OF ONE TO TEN.
TEN...TEN...TEN...TEN...TEN...TEN... TEN...TEN...TEN...TEN...TEN...TEN... TEN...TEN...TEN...TEN...TEN...TEN... TEN...TEN...TEN...TEN...TEN...TEN... TEN...TEN...TEN...TEN...TEN...TEN...
IT'S BEEN A GOOD MONTH.

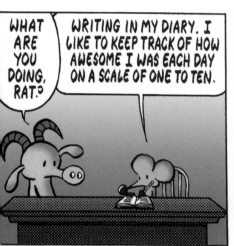

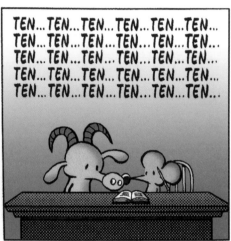

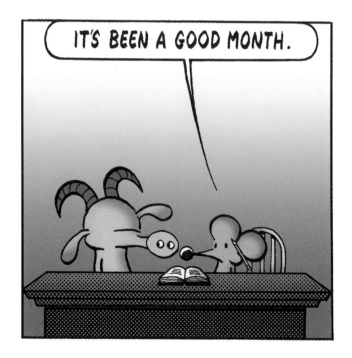

HEY, RAT...THIS IS MY FRIEND, SCIENTIST BOB. HE DOES FIELD RESEARCH INTO THE SOUNDS MADE BY DIFFERENT SPECIES OF ANIMALS.
HOW'S HE DO THAT?
PULL
The cow says 'Moooooooooo.'
I QUESTION HIS METHODOLOGY.

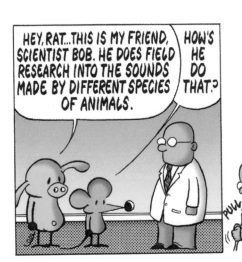

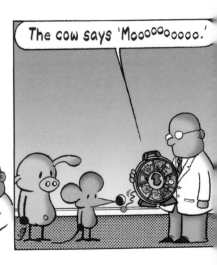

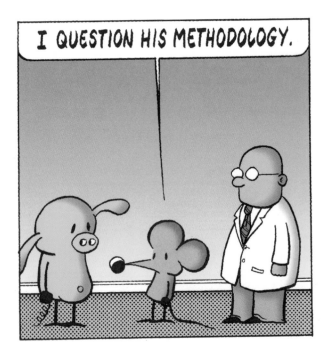

Zeeba neighba...Look out weendow. Ees thundering hoofs of hundred zeeba migrating cross Serengeti. Come outside...Join you peeple...
Hoof Hoof Hoof Hoof Hoof Hoof
You drawings not dat photo-realistic, Larry.
Hey. Zeeba hoofs no go 'HOOF HOOF,' Bob.

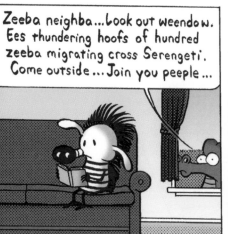

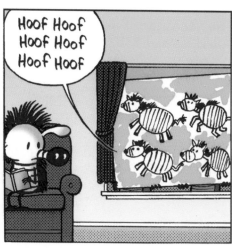

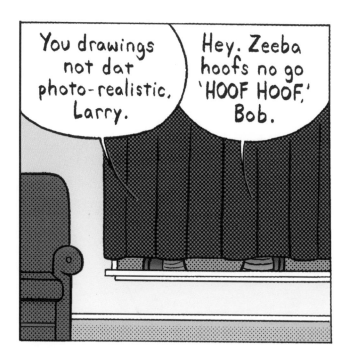

Hey, son, want feesh wid me and Bob? Lake s'pose have huge feesh.
WHAT ARE YOU GUYS USING FOR BAIT?
Bob.
You made me miss feesh.

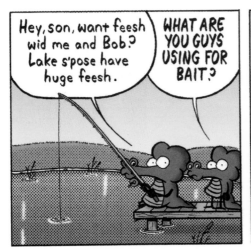

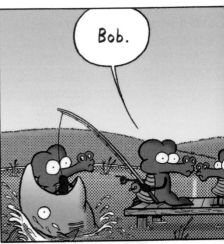

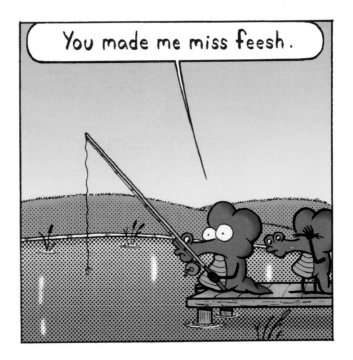

HEY, GOAT ...I'VE GOT A QUESTION, BUT IT'S KIND OF COMPLEX, SO CAN YOU WAIT 'TIL I'M DONE BEFORE YOU ANSWER?
SURE.
ALRIGHT, SO IF A GUY IS FROM AMERICA, YOU SAY HE'S AMERICAN. AND IF A GUY IS FROM RUSSIA, YOU SAY HE'S RUSSIAN. BUT IF THE GUY IS FROM FINLAND, YOU SAY HE'S WHAT?
FINNISH.
I DID.
DID WHAT?
YOU'RE NOT VERY HELPFUL.

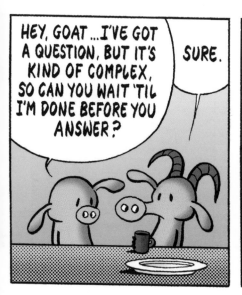

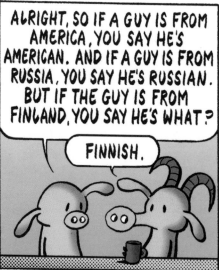

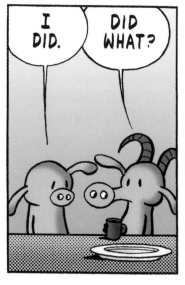

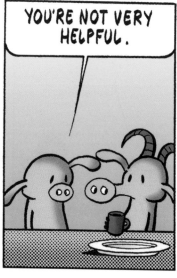

WHAT ARE YOU LOOKING AT, GOAT?
HEY, PIG. MAYBE YOU CAN HELP ME...I'M TRYING TO PICK A VIVARIUM. I'M GONNA BUY A SNAKE AND I NEED A PLACE FOR HIM TO LIVE.
ONLY $1700
THEN WHY A VIVARIUM?
BECAUSE IT'S WHERE YOU KEEP SNAKES.
I THOUGHT IT'S WHERE YOU KEPT VIVIANS.
MAYBE I DON'T NEED YOUR HELP.
OHHHH, MY AUNT VIVIAN WOULD NEVER FIT IN THIS.

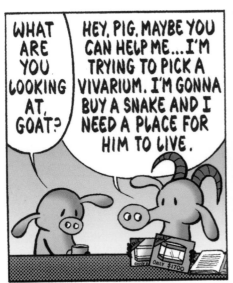

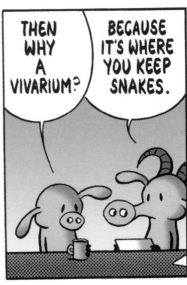

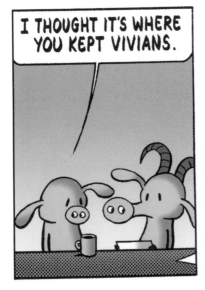

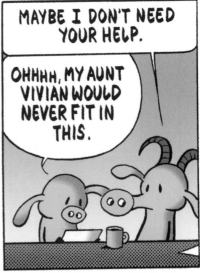

WHERE WERE YOU THIS MORNING?
FILLING OUT MY CALENDAR FOR THE MONTH. I LIKE TO KEEP ON TOP OF MY SOCIAL SCHEDULE.
OH, YEAH? WHAT EVENTS DO YOU HAVE COMING UP?
NEXT TUESDAY IS THE EXPIRATION DATE ON MY MILK.
YOU MIGHT WANT TO GET OUT MORE.
WHOA...SAME DAY AS THE CHEESE... GONNA BE A BUSY TUESDAY.

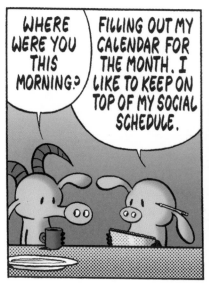

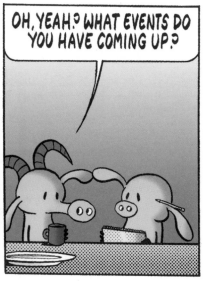

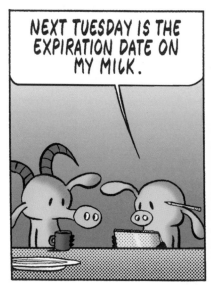

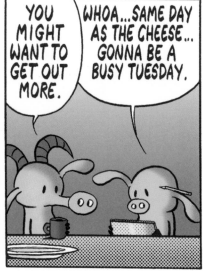

HEY, PIG, I'D LIKE YOU TO MEET MY FRIEND, IRA GLASS. HE'S THE HOST OF MY FAVORITE RADIO SHOW, 'THIS AMERICAN LIFE.'
HI... IT'S REALLY NICE TO—
FIRE! FIRE!

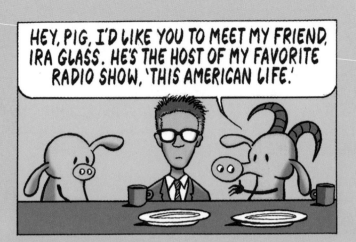

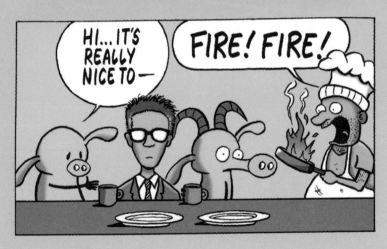

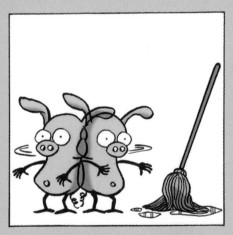

WHAM
WHAM
PIG! PIG! WHAT THE HECK ARE YOU—
IN CASE OF EMERGENCY
BREAK GLASS
HEY... FIRE'S OUT.
I'M A HERO.
I AM SO, SO SORRY.

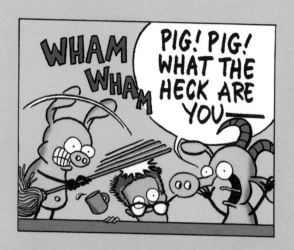

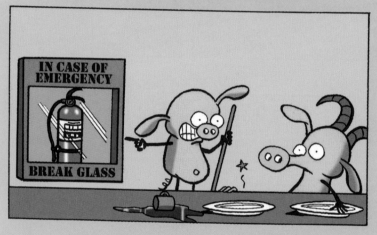

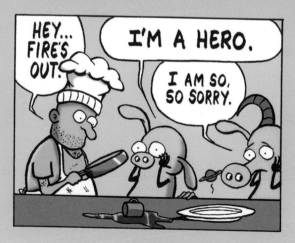

HEY, RAT, LOOK AT ME. I'M A BEEKEEPER! I EVEN GOT THE NET THING THAT THE BEES CAN'T GET THROUGH.
WHERE ARE THE BEES?
IN HERE.
OW!
YOU'D THINK THERE'D BE A BETTER WAY.

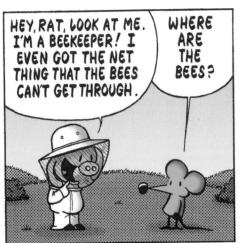

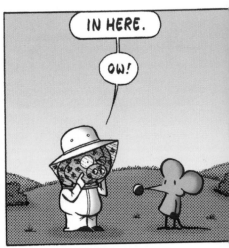

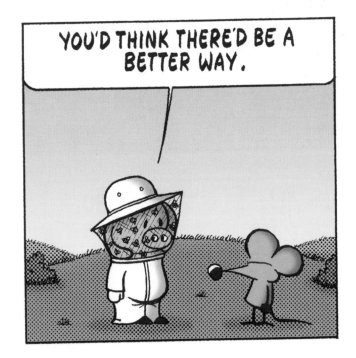

HEY, PIG, WHAT ARE YOU DOING?
I'M WRITING A LETTER TO THE HOST OF THIS CABLE NEWS SHOW. HIS DISCUSSION OF AN ISSUE WAS SO UNFAIR.
GOOD FOR YOU, PIG...IT'S CRITICAL IN A DEMOCRACY THAT CITIZENS ENGAGE IN THE PROCESS BY DEBATING ISSUES THOUGHTFULLY WITH OTHERS. HERE, LET ME SEE WHAT YOU HAVE SO FAR.
Dear Poopyhead
PERHAPS I COULD BE THOUGHTFUL-ER.

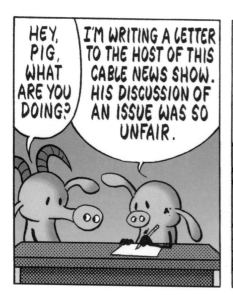

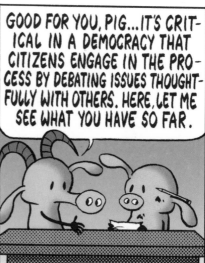

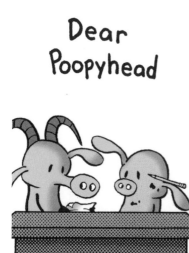

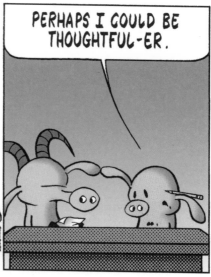

HEY, NEIGHBOR BOB... HOW'S YOUR SON, WILLY?
OH, GREAT, PIG. HE JUST TURNED TWELVE AND STARTED SEVENTH GRADE.
TWELVE, HUH? WHAT A WONDERFUL AGE! YOU'VE GOT FRIENDS, SOCCER, VIDEO GAMES, SUMMER CAMP...IS HE ENJOYING IT ALL?
OH, YEAH...AND ALL I'VE ASKED HIM TO DO IS TO MAKE SURE HE MAINTAINS A PERFECT 4.0.
YAAAAY, CHILDHOOD.
OH... ...HI, WILLY.
SHHHH. HE WON'T GET INTO YALE.

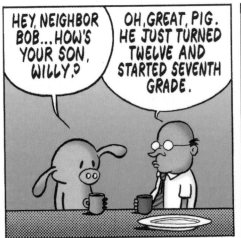

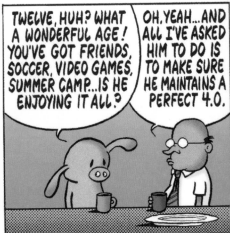

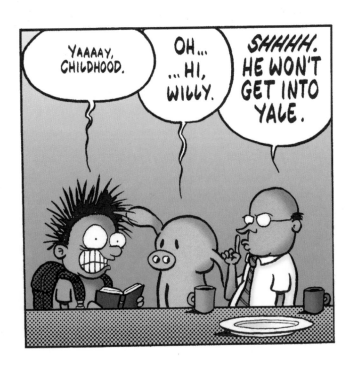

DID YOU KNOW THAT SPIDERS KILL THEIR PREY BY INJECTING THEM WITH VENOM AND SUCKING OUT THEIR INSIDES WITH THIS LONG APPENDAGE CALLED A PROBOSCIS?
REALLY?
REALLY. HAVE YOU EVER HEARD OF ANYTHING SO GROSS?
NEVER.
WILL YOU PLEASE STOP DOING THAT EVERY TIME I DRINK A SMOOTHIE?
WHOA. SORRY, MAN. DIDN'T SEE YOU THERE.
I WILL NOT BE ORDERING THAT.

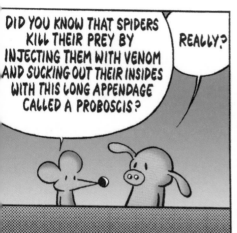

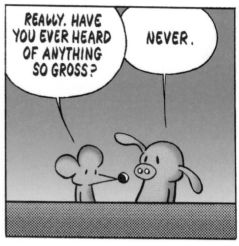

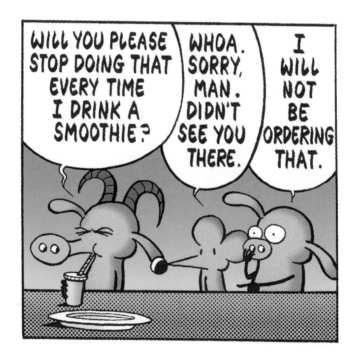

HEY, GOAT... WHERE YOU OFF TO?
I NEED SOME GREETING CARDS, SO I'M GOING TO THAT NEW STATIONERY STORE.
WAS THE OLD ONE ROLLING AROUND?
NEVER MIND.
I PREFER ALL MY STORES TO BE STATIONARY.

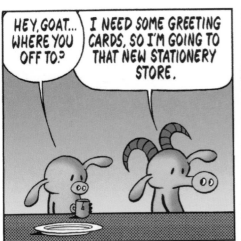

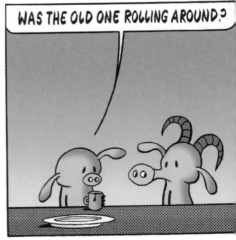

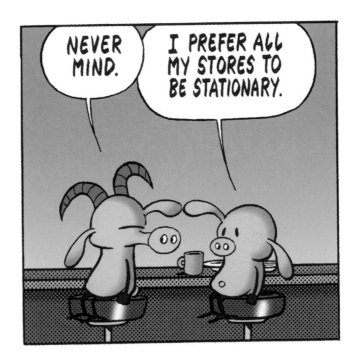

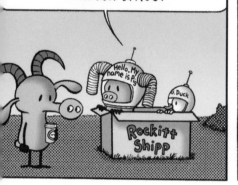

HEY, GOAT, WANT TO COME WITH ME AND GUARD DUCK ON OUR JOURNEY THROUGH SPACE?
Hello. My name is Pig
G. Duck
Rockitt Shipp
HAHAHA... WELL, GOSH, PIG, I'D LOVE TO PLAY WITH YOU TWO IN THAT BIG CARDBOARD BOX, BUT I'VE GOTTA RUN TO THE BANK... SO YOU GUYS HAVE FUN.
Hello. My name is Pig
G. Duck
Rockitt Shipp
HE LOOKED SURPRISED WHEN THE ROCKET BOOSTERS KICKED IN.
G. Duck
Rockitt Shipp

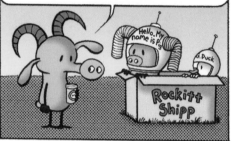

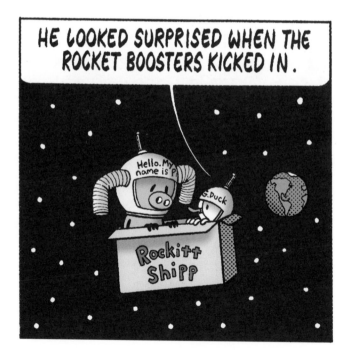

ALRIGHT, SUPPLY OFFICER DUCK, NOW THAT WE'RE IN SPACE, WE SHOULD GO THROUGH OUR 'THREE ESSENTIAL ITEMS CHECKLIST.'... LET'S SEE.... PEANUT BUTTER?
CHECK.
ROOT BEER?
CHECK.
OXYGEN SUPPLY?
Rockitt Shipp
G. Duck
IT'S VERY TASTY PEANUT BUTTER.
Rockitt Shipp

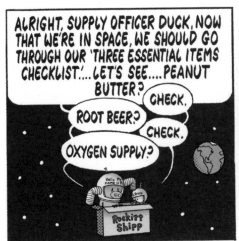

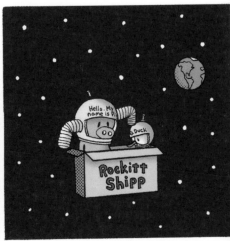

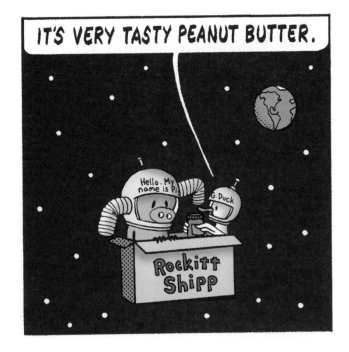

Hey. Whuh dis stoopid wall doing here?
IT'S MORE PROTECTION FROM YOU PREDATORS.
Who want talk staring over stoopid wall?
STILL MISSING YOU, SPARKY...
MIND KEEPING IT DOWN?

Who Meester Beeg Head?

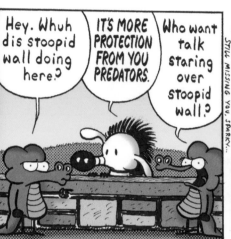

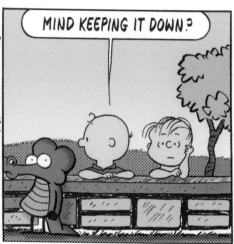

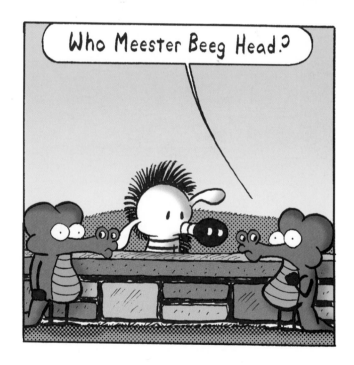

Ohhh...Me could catch heem.
Yeah. Me could catch too.
Me could tear off dat guy head.
Yeah. Me would reep to shred.

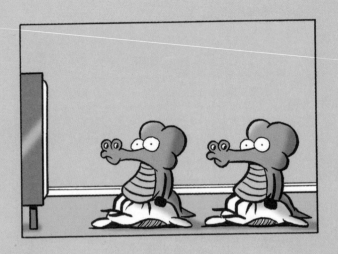

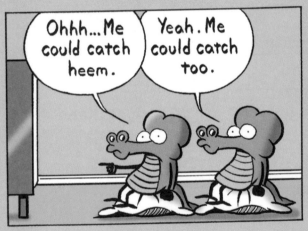

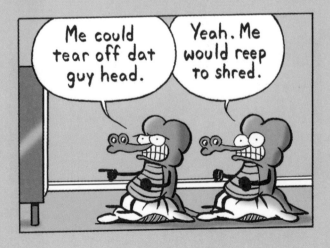

Ooooh, me could so keel dat one!
Yeah, me would eet in seconds!
DAD, I KNOW YOU AND BOB ARE TOUGH, BUT YOU MAKE IT REALLY HARD TO WATCH 'THE MUPPETS.'
Told you dat not nature documentary.

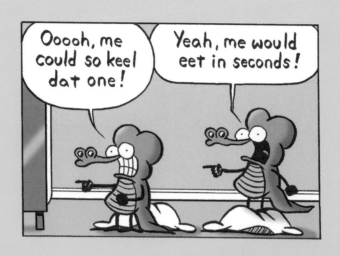

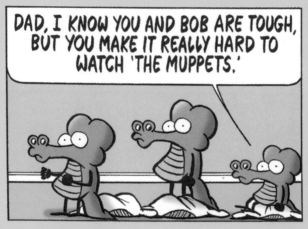

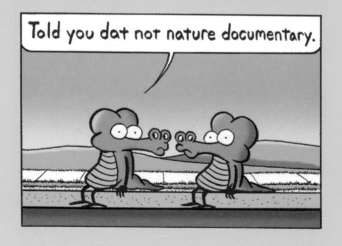

HEY, NEIGHBOR BOB, WHATEVER HAPPENED TO YOUR HAIR?
OH, I LOST IT YEARS AGO.
DO YOU KNOW WHERE YOU LEFT IT LAST?
HAVE YOU TRIED RE-TRACING YOUR STEPS?
LET'S STOP TALKING.

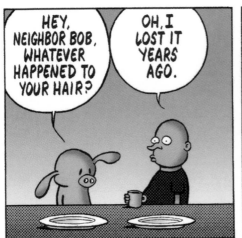

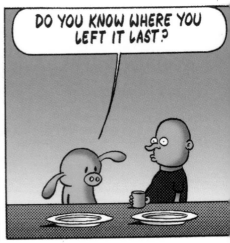

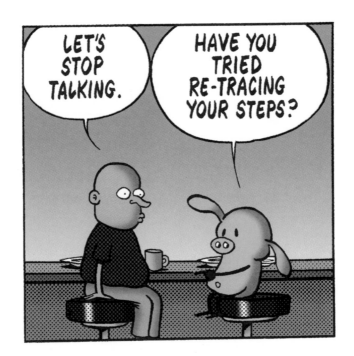

WHAT ARE YOU DOING, RAT?
PIG TICKED ME OFF THIS MORNING SO I'M HOLDING A GRUDGE AS A MEANS OF GETTING HIM BACK.
SKIP SKIP SKIP
YOU'RE REALLY AFFECTING HIM.
HAHA HAAA... TAKE *THAT*, YOU STUPID PIG!

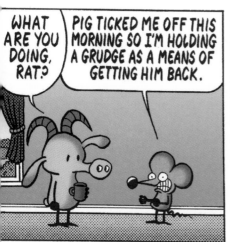

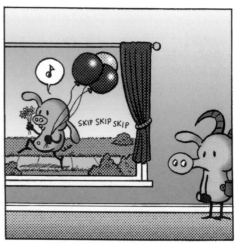

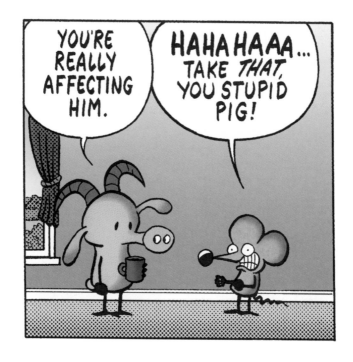

WHAT DO YOU GOT THERE, RAT?
ACOUSTIC TILES. PEOPLE USE THEM ON RESTAURANT CEILINGS AND STUFF TO ABSORB SOUND. THAT WAY YOU DON'T HAVE TO HEAR ALL THE CHATTER FROM THE IDIOTS SITTING AT THE NEXT TABLE.
BUT I LIKE HEARING THAT CHATTER. IT'S HOW I LEARN THINGS AND MEET A LOT OF NEW PEOPLE.
THIS WILL IMPROVE OUR FRIENDSHIP.

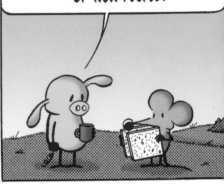

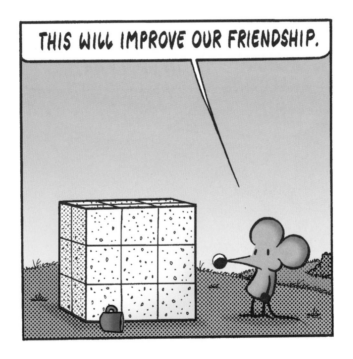

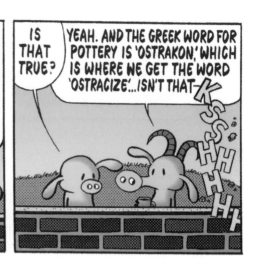

DID YOU KNOW THE ANCIENT GREEKS HAD A TRADITION OF BREAKING POTTERY AND GIVING EACH CITIZEN A SHARD ON WHICH THEY COULD WRITE THE NAME OF ONE GUY THEY WANTED TO KICK OUT OF THE CITY? WHOEVER GOT THE MOST VOTES WAS EXILED.

IS THAT TRUE?

YEAH. AND THE GREEK WORD FOR POTTERY IS 'OSTRAKON,' WHICH IS WHERE WE GET THE WORD 'OSTRACIZE'...ISN'T THAT—

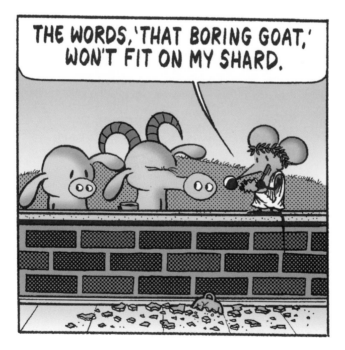

THE WORDS, 'THAT BORING GOAT,' WON'T FIT ON MY SHARD.

WHAT ARE YOU DOING, RAT?
I HAVE STUMBLED UPON A FORM OF COMMUNICATION THAT IS SO CAREFULLY ENCODED I CAN ONLY ASSUME IT WAS ACCIDENTALLY DROPPED HERE BY ALIENS.
Dw i ddim yn gwybod.
Ydw.
Mae'n ddrwg gen i.
THAT'S WELSH.
DO YOU SUPPOSE THEY COME IN PEACE?

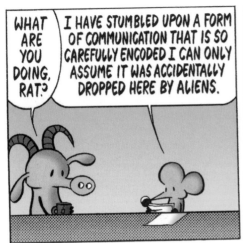

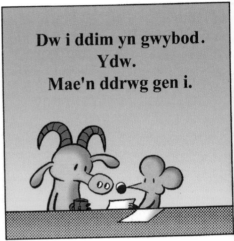

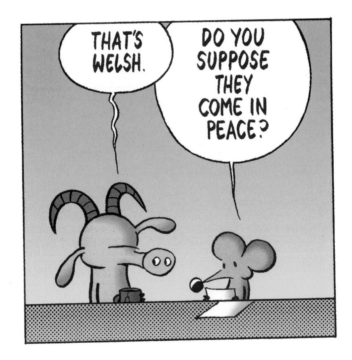

HEY, RAT, IT'S ME, ZEBRA. YOU SEEN PIG?
NOPE. WE WENT TO THE PARK LAST WEEK TO PLAY 'HIDE AND SEEK,' BUT I HAVEN'T DONE ANYTHING WITH HIM SINCE.
FOUND YOU.

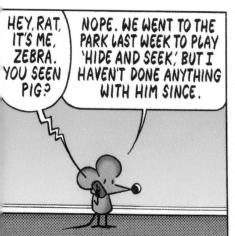

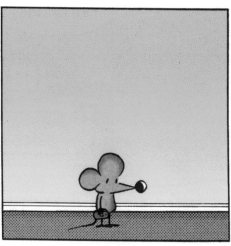

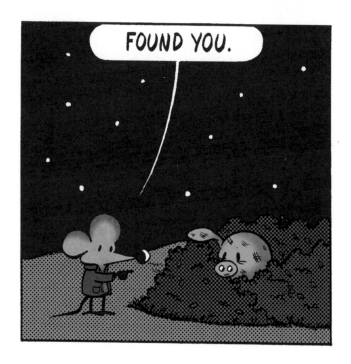

HEY, NEIGHBOR WILLY! WANT TO FLY TO MARS?
CAN'T. HAVE TO STUDY.
Hello, My Name is Pig
Rockitt Shipp
WHY?
I NEED A 4.6 G.P.A.
WHAT FOR?
Hello, My Name is Pig
Rockitt Shipp
TO GET INTO A TOP-TIER, IVY LEAGUE SCHOOL.
WHERE, IF I WORK REALLY HARD, I CAN GET A DEGREE AND THEN A SIX-FIGURE JOB.
WHERE, IF I WORK EVEN HARDER, I CAN MAKE A LOT OF MONEY FOR MANY YEARS.

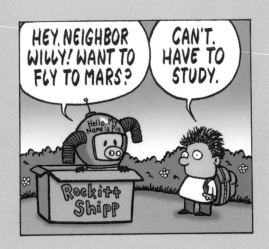

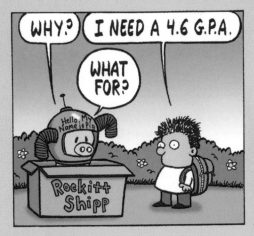

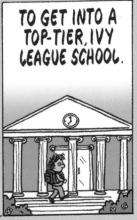

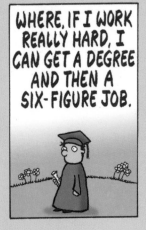

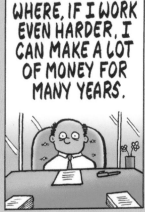

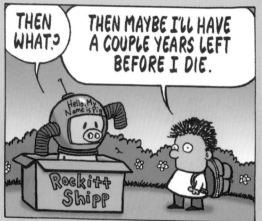

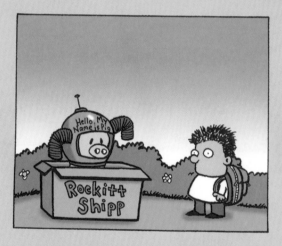

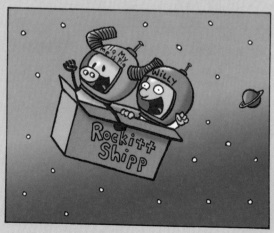

Pearls Before Swine is distributed internationally by Universal Uclick.

Skip School, Fly to Space copyright © 2015 by Stephan Pastis. All rights reserved. Printed in China. No part of this book may be used or reproduced in any manner whatsoever without written permission except in the case of reprints in the context of reviews.

Andrews McMeel Publishing, LLC
an Andrews McMeel Universal company
1130 Walnut Street, Kansas City, Missouri 64106

www.andrewsmcmeel.com

15 16 17 18 19 SDB 10 9 8 7 6 5 4 3 2 1

ISBN: 978-1-4494-3637-7

Library of Congress Control Number: 2015931761

Pearls Before Swine can be viewed on the Internet at www.pearlscomic.com.

Made by:
Shenzen Donnelley Printing Company Ltd.
Address and location of manufacturer:
No. 47, Wuhe Nan Road, Bantian Ind. Zone,
Shenzhen China, 518129
1st Printing – 5/18/15

ATTENTION: SCHOOLS AND BUSINESSES

Andrews McMeel books are available at quantity discounts with bulk purchase for educational, business, or sales promotional use. For information, please e-mail the Andrews McMeel Publishing Special Sales Department: specialsales@amuniversal.com.

Be sure to check out other *Pearls Before Swine* AMP! Comics for Kids books and others at ampkids.com.

BEGINNING PEARLS
Stephan T. Pastis
New York Times Bestselling Author
THE CROC ATE MY HOMEWORK
New York Times Bestselling Author
Stephan T. Pastis
A Pearls Before Swine Collection

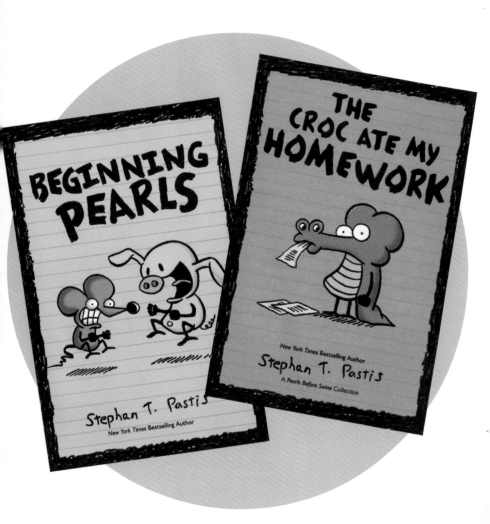

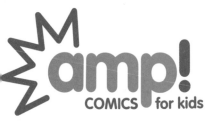
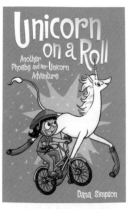
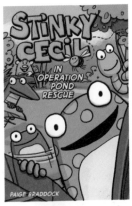
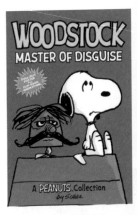
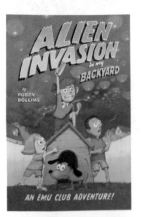
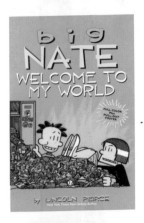
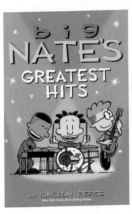
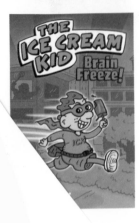
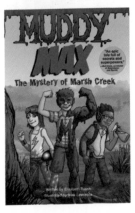
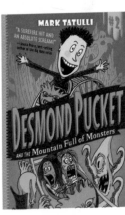

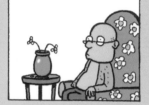

WHICH, IF EVERY-THING GOES RIGHT, WILL ALLOW ME TO RETIRE COMFORTABLY AT 65.
THEN WHAT?
THEN MAYBE I'LL HAVE A COUPLE YEARS LEFT BEFORE I DIE.
Hello, My Name is Pig
Rockitt Shipp
Hello, My Name is Pig
Rockitt Shipp
Willy
Rockitt Shipp

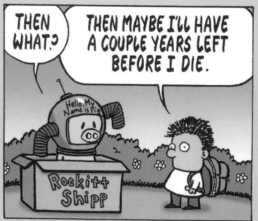

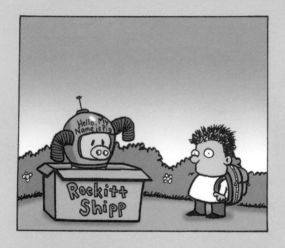

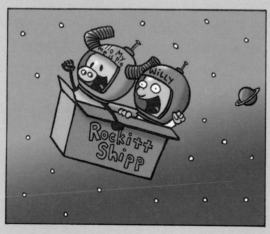

Pearls Before Swine is distributed internationally by Universal Uclick.

Skip School, Fly to Space copyright © 2015 by Stephan Pastis. All rights reserved. Printed in China. No part of this book may be used or reproduced in any manner whatsoever without written permission except in the case of reprints in the context of reviews.

Andrews McMeel Publishing, LLC
an Andrews McMeel Universal company
1130 Walnut Street, Kansas City, Missouri 64106

www.andrewsmcmeel.com

15 16 17 18 19 SDB 10 9 8 7 6 5 4 3 2 1

ISBN: 978-1-4494-3637-7

Library of Congress Control Number: 2015931761

Pearls Before Swine can be viewed on the Internet at www.pearlscomic.com.

Made by:
Shenzen Donnelley Printing Company Ltd.
Address and location of manufacturer:
No. 47, Wuhe Nan Road, Bantian Ind. Zone,
Shenzhen China, 518129
1st Printing – 5/18/15

ATTENTION: SCHOOLS AND BUSINESSES

Andrews McMeel books are available at quantity discounts with bulk purchase for educational, business, or sales promotional use. For information, please e-mail the Andrews McMeel Publishing Special Sales Department: specialsales@amuniversal.com.

Be sure to check out other *Pearls Before Swine* AMP! Comics for Kids books and others at ampkids.com.

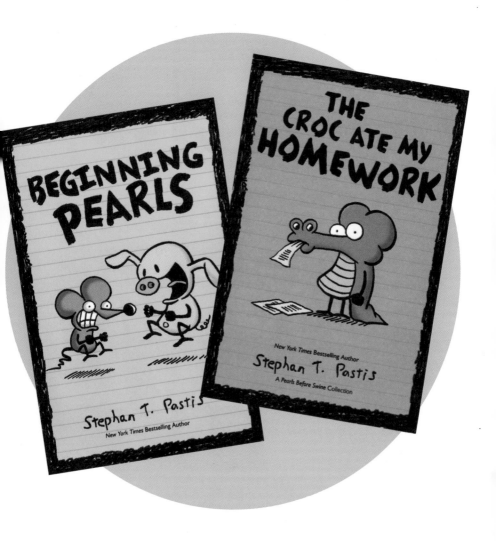

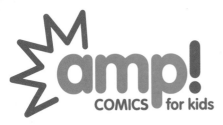

Check out these and other books at ampkids.com

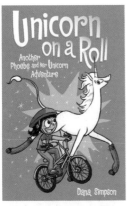

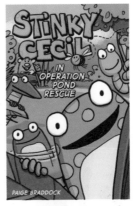

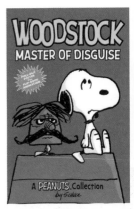

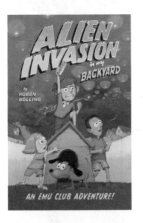

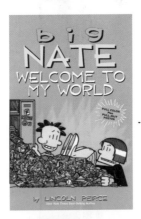

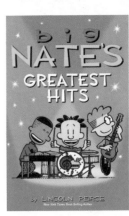

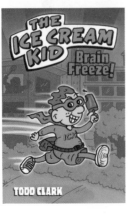

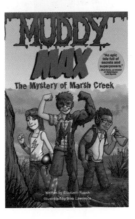

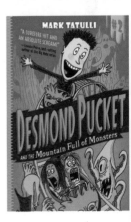

Also available:
Teaching and activity guides for each title.
AMP! Comics for Kids books make reading FUN!